The Yellow House on Maloney Grove

M. Bryce Ternet

Copyright © 2015 M. Bryce Ternet
All rights reserved.
Second Edition. First Published
2012, United States of America.

To Renata & Bryce

Prologue

At first glance, the little yellow house on Maloney Grove looked like a place where we would happily start our family; it was like watching a dream come true. I could see our future children playing outside in the back yard while my husband cooked food on the big fancy gas grill we would buy someday. I imagined watching the kids play while I flipped through the pages of a magazine. At night, we would all nestle on the couch and watch television, the children gently falling asleep on our laps. Of course, I let myself get carried away and romanticized it all a little, but it just seemed like a good fit for us.

I told Ethan on our first viewing of the house that I loved it and wanted it. We looked at a few other rental properties around town after, but I was fixated on the yellow house. On our second visit to the house, I saw from the look on his face that he was as excited as I was about it. We didn't always agree, as I expected most husbands and wives did not, but we did tend to find compromise in our marriage. Normally the compromise leaned more in my direction, but thankfully, Ethan didn't seem to mind. I knew he loved me dearly and enjoyed seeing me pleased. I felt completely content to share my life with him, and I was glad to call him my husband. Moving into this little old house was a jump start into the next step of our relationship.

The Realtor showing us the house seemed courteous and tried to answer any questions we posed. When we met her on our first viewing of the house, she asked that we call her Maul, which was a bit curious to me, as the name on her business card was "Cynthia Dixon." Ethan had commented to me earlier as we followed her around town viewing rental houses that in all of his previous correspondence with her over email, he had not encountered the nickname, either. Perhaps it was just her middle name or nickname? But why would someone prefer to go by a name like Maul instead of Cynthia? In my experience, people often did such things to reinvent themselves. Maybe she had done something that she felt guilty about and wanted to forget?

But she was nice enough and had the sort of bubbly personality that made you feel comforted in her presence. We hadn't had much experience with Realtors, but I thought their reputation for being slimy was unfair. Maul appeared very honest.

"Oh, just look how cute this exposed brick is here in this room!" Maul exclaimed as we followed her into a small room located in between the living room and kitchen. "And this wood burning stove is a genuine article; it's actually from the original house." She paused for a moment and then asked for the second time, "It's just the two of you, right?"

"Yes, just us," Ethan responded and then changed the subject. "And when was the house built?" Ethan asked; he was always interested in history.

"Around 1920, so nearly a hundred years ago! And I promise that once winter comes and you start using it, this stove is going to cook you out!" Maul added excitedly.

I didn't understand what "cook you out" meant. I didn't really like the sound of it, but figured it was just something one said in the area and didn't want to ask a dumb question. But we'd never lived in a house with a wood burning stove, and it sounded cozy and romantic. I must say, though, that it felt like winter had already begun at the end of October. Since we had arrived in Washington State on our house hunting trip, I'd been freezing!

"It would be just the two of you moving in, right?" Maul asked for the third time.

****

Why did Mrs. Maul, my new name for her, keep asking questions like that? I'd told her in my initial inquiry emails that it was just the two of us. Once we began to show real interest in this particular house, though, Mrs. Maul persisted in confirming that it really would be just the two of us.

I liked Mrs. Maul and all, but our family plans were none of her damned business. It was actually starting to creep me out a bit, the more I thought about it. She agreed to take us through the house for a second viewing. I had a strong feeling that she was interested in knowing if and when we were planning to have any children. I guessed that she was not supposed to ask us straight out, as that could have been grounds for discrimination, but she was making her point loud and clear, to me anyway. Libby didn't seem to notice this slight weirdness about Mrs. Maul, and considering how happy Libby looked, I decided to let it go. Maybe the property owners had pressured Mrs. Maul about discouraging renters with children for some strange reason. Mrs. Maul had told us the house was owned by a very wealthy couple. Rich people were odd…probably explanation enough.

I knew Libby really wanted the house, so I kept answering in a way that I thought would please Mrs. Maul. I seized the opportunity as I followed her into the master bedroom while Libby lagged behind checking out the kitchen's expansive cabinet space, repeating what I had already said numerous times before. "Yup, just us. No kids, and we're not planning on that changing anytime soon," I offered, safely out of range of Libby overhearing. Which was a total lie, as Libby wanted to have children as soon as possible.

Mrs. Maul turned and grinned at me, nodding her head in approval. She was pleased with the response.

Chapter 1

October

The day of our arrival to the new house was not as glamorous as I had hoped it would be. First off, we were so tired after driving the U-Haul truck the entire day through southern Oregon all the way up to North Bend, Washington, that we didn't have any energy to unload the truck, so we had an empty house for the night that suddenly somehow felt spooky to me. I didn't want to say anything to Ethan about it; he'd driven most of the way, and he looked exhausted. I also knew that deep down, he didn't really want to leave San Diego. But after we both finished our respective graduate school programs at USD, we agreed that we would move wherever one of us found a promising job first. So I'd accepted a position in Seattle with a prominent insurance company. It wasn't the best pay in the world, but the benefits were outstanding and, well, especially these days…it was a job.

It was Saturday evening, and I started my new position on Monday. Dinner consisted of a grocery store-bought roasted chicken and a loaf of thick bread. Not the best, but considering we hadn't unpacked any kitchen items, we were a bit limited on cooking options. We sipped on a cheap bottle of wine that Ethan picked up with the food, and I was grateful for the slight warmth it provided. We were seated on our blow up mattress we use for camping in the living room, watching a movie on my laptop.

The night had turned frigid, and the air in the house was freezing. Instead of complaining, I just crawled inside of my sleeping bag and pretended to be interested in the movie (I really wasn't; Ethan picked it out). We hadn't had sex in a while; the stress of the move really turned me off from the idea, and I believed it was the same for him, if that was actually possible with men. I glanced over at Ethan and could see that he was thoroughly engaged in the movie. *Another time.*

But the house was seriously cold. I didn't know it could be so cold at the end of October. In San Diego, October was an incredible time of the year for weather: crystal clear blue skies and temperatures in the mid-seventies. I decided to try to sleep and not think about it too much. I imagined I would get accustomed to the new climate eventually. As I closed my eyes and rested my head on the pillow, I couldn't help but notice that I didn't feel the same sense of joy that I felt when we first viewed the house. Maybe it was because the sun was out at those times, instead of dark and dreary like it had been. That had to be it. The next day would be better.

* * * *

Libby often fell asleep when we watched movies together at night. I thought it was cute, but I didn't know how she could sleep through action-packed films. The only way I knew if she liked a movie or not was if she asked me in the morning how it ended.

We hadn't really driven around the town much yet. When the sky was clear, we had a real sense of being surrounded by mountains, and I hoped that it would be like that again soon. It had been beautiful when we first visited on our house hunting trip a few weeks earlier. The day that we first viewed the house with Mrs. Maul, it was pretty amazing to notice how close we were to North Bend's famous Mt. Si. On a clear day, it was like right there! The base of the distinct mountain must have been at most a half mile from the house. It loomed over the house like it was watching over us. But the area wasn't nearly quite as special without all those ridge lines and peaks. It was just bleak without them.

Although I thought the house would feel much better once we got everything unpacked and set up. Until then, it would just be empty space and hardwood floors. While I was watching the movie, I heard strange noises once in a while. But it was pretty windy outside, so I figured the old house was just creaking.

* * * *

What the hell was that noise? The room was completely dark, and Ethan was soundly asleep next to me in his sleeping bag, but I swore I heard something. I didn't normally wake up easily, but I'd heard something!

A cold chill pulsated through me as I laid my head back down on the pillow. I tried to close my eyes, but they instantly shot open once again, staring into the darkness above me. And what was the smell I just noticed? I really hoped I'd get used to living in this house...

* * * *

"Hey, Lib! Come over here and check this out!" I called to Libby. She stepped into the guest bedroom, in her favorite pair of torn jeans and a baggy hooded sweatshirt. Back in San Diego she would wear those jeans with a tank top, showing off her tanned arms and her equally tanned legs through the various tears in the jeans. Without fail, that look turned me on. Considering that it was a chilly fifty degrees outside, I wasn't surprised she'd covered those sexy arms in a hoodie.

"What is it?" she asked.

I pointed out the window to where a small rabbit happily chomped on some grass in the house's small front yard area. "Looks like the house comes with our own pet bunny."

"Ah, it's so cute!" Libby agreed. "When we go to the store, let's get some carrots to toss out to it. We should give it a name. Why don't you do it; you're good with coming up with names."

I considered it for a moment and then responded: "Mrs. Pendergrass."

Libby shook her head with a smile and leaned over to kiss me. "My creative husband; I have no idea where you come up with things sometimes," she said to me before leaving the room with a wide grin on her face. "For now, Mrs. Pendergrass is on her own, though. We have a lot of work to do getting moved into this place!" she called from some other room.

I smiled at Mrs. Pendergrass and then returned to carrying boxes into the house from the U-Haul truck parked in the driveway. As I turned away, I noticed that there was one of those small plastic scent infused containers on the window sill. I then looked over at the other window and saw that there was one there, as well. I guess I noticed them when Mrs. Maul was showing us the house, but as I thought more about it, they were everywhere. Was our landlord so concerned that the house smelled bad? Maybe the previous renters smoked or something? I hoped that without them, the house wouldn't stink. Libby had an acute sense of smell.

I supposed I could have asked Mrs. Maul about it, but maybe not. We had yet to meet our new landlord. In fact, the whole arrangement with Mrs. Maul felt a little strange. She worked for a realty and property management company, but she'd made it clear, repeatedly, that she was not our property manager. Instead we would deal directly and exclusively with the house's owner as landlord. Mrs. Maul must have said this to us at least five times, as if she'd wanted to make it crystal clear that once we signed the lease, we were no longer going to have any contact with her. We knew that meant any issues we encountered with the house would have to be addressed with the owner.

It bothered me slightly that Mrs. Maul also kept repeating, in one way or another, that she wouldn't be our actual property manager. This made me think that Mrs. Maul was providing the groundwork to be automatically disassociated with any complications we may have in the future; it also seemed that by saying this to us, she was trying to ease her own conscience in an "I can't be blamed" sort of way. What did she expect would happen?

All the same, we had signed a year lease, and I didn't see us moving anytime soon. Actually, I doubted we'd be able to afford it anyway. We were both racked with student loan repayments and mounting credit card debt. This move ended up costing us a lot more than we anticipated. Libby's new job had a decent salary that could carry us for a while, but I still needed to find a job. Considering the economy was far from spectacular, I expected it to take some time.

Besides, maybe I was being overly cautious. Apprehensive, like Lib always said. The house was fine.

I looked outside again and saw that it had started raining again.

* * * *

Of course, Ethan and I expected it to rain a lot…We'd moved to the Seattle area, after all. And we'd been looking forward to the change. We were excited to have some sort of seasonal variety, and I thought the rainy climate would be kind of fun. It would just encourage us to spend more time cuddled on the couch together, which was something I never got enough of.

But I wasn't expecting it to be so chilly so soon. I figured we would have at least have a few weeks before it turned really cold, but the house was truthfully already really frigid! I think it was actually warmer outside. How could that be?

My parents had told me that we should never use the floorboard space heaters in the house. Apparently they were extremely pricey and inefficient. Coming from a place where we never once turned on the heat, the thought of high electricity bills frightened us. Our lease indicated that we needed to buy our own wood for the stove. Maul recommended that would be the most cost effective way to heat the home. And, of course, we were assured that the wood burning stove would "cook us out!" Whatever that meant...

Perhaps the chill was because of the damp weather and lack of sun. We hadn't started looking for firewood yet; we didn't even have internet access in the house, and I couldn't find any network to jump on with my laptop, but I planned to ask Ethan to find us our winter wood supply soon. Even just saying it, "winter wood supply," sounded so romantic!

* * * *

I wondered if Lib was asleep on her side of the bed. The sound of the rain pelting the roof was more noticeable in the bedroom than in any other room of the house. It was a soft, steady drum roll that just kept beating against the roof. Before we turned out the night stand light, Libby commented on how hearing the rain reminded her of camping trips when we had been rained on while in our tent.

We'd spent all day moving in boxes and furniture from the truck, and the place felt more like a maze of towering box piles than a house. At least we were able to get the bedroom set up. It had been an exhausting day for sure. Libby started her new job in the morning, and I would start arranging the house. I hoped she was able to get some sleep, as I knew she was a bit nervous about starting her job. I was afraid to move too much because I didn't want to wake her, but I couldn't sleep. I just stared at the ceiling.

I would have been staring into darkness, but the neighbors had a powerful flood light on their garage, which shined directly into our bedroom. Lib wasn't happy about this at all. I needed to figure out a way to at least temporarily get the windows behind our heads covered until we put up a more permanent solution.

Our master bedroom was unique, though. All the walls and ceiling had wood siding, with a hardwood floor like the rest of the house, so it looked like a room of a log cabin. Once we got the windows taken care of, it would be a nice room.

I didn't detect the odd smell as much in there as in other rooms of the house, so that was good, too. From time to time, I thought I heard something scurry in the ceiling. Great...mice. I hoped Libby didn't hear it. She'd freak out.

I remembered that I'd noticed earlier what appeared to be an attic above the main frame of the house. I'd searched throughout the house but wasn't able to find any kind of access to it. The only way to get up there seemed to be through a small window at the front of the house. The problem was that the window was a good ten feet up, and we didn't have a ladder. I'd joked with Lib when I showed her the window, calling it a "secret window."

The mouse, or whatever it was, scurried again above us.

* * * *

Shit, Lib wasn't going to be happy. She was not the most patient person. The only internet provider servicing the area told me that a technician couldn't get out here to get us hooked up until late in the week. The operator informed me that the installer had to drive all the way from Renton to get here, as if this was some sort of excuse. I didn't even know where the hell Renton was in relation to North Bend.

Since I couldn't do anything more about the internet connection, I decided that I would try to find us some firewood.

* * * *

"Hello, Maul, this Ethan Peterson from the house over on Maloney Grove." I expected Mrs. Maul to say something in response, but she remained silent. I tried to prod her memory. "My wife, Libby, and I just rented the house from you a couple of weeks ago over here on Maloney Grove…"

"Oh, yes," she responded.

"Well, I was just calling because—" I started before she cut me off.

"But just to be clear, you didn't rent the house from me; you rented it from the owners. I was only hired by them to facilitate finding suitable renters for the property," she hurriedly corrected.

Okay…weird, I thought. "Sure, I'm aware of that. Anyway, I was just calling because when you showed us the house, you mentioned thinking we could easily find firewood by driving around town. But I've driven around quite a bit and haven't seen anything." I also suddenly remembered that Mrs. Maul told us when she first showed us the place that she would be sure to call us with names of a few places where we could buy wood, which she never did.

"You're just new here and don't know where to look," she responded.

I told myself to not feel at all offended by the curtness of the remark. I was calling to ask for her assistance, after all, and she had offered it. I decided to try to lighten the conversation by laughing a little. "I'm sure that's true, but I was hoping you may be able to point me in the right direction?"

Mrs. Maul sighed heavily, as if I'd requested something ridiculously inconvenient. "Listen, I'm really busy today, but I'll get back to you later."

Mrs. Maul hung up before I was able to give her my cell number. She only had Lib's phone, but Libby told me that her new job wasn't a personal phone call friendly environment.

I got back to unpacking and trying to arrange our little house. Rain poured down, and fierce winds blew small branches against the side of the house.

When Libby returned from work, she told me that she received no call from Mrs. Maul.

* * * *

I called Mrs. Maul the next morning and got her voicemail. I left a polite message requesting possible firewood contacts. Not long after I hung up, Libby called while on her lunch break.

"Have you talked to Mrs. Maul about the wood yet?" she pointedly asked.

"Hi, Libby," I calmly replied.

"Sorry, Ethan; I didn't mean to be rude. But I'd really like you to get wood soon. It sucks arriving home from work to a cold house."

She had made that comment before. It hadn't stopped dumping rain in two days, and the winds had only grown stronger the entire time; the combination with a lack of sunshine was bone chilling. She had a point, but it was still annoying.

I tried calling Mrs. Maul again. This time, she answered.

"Hi, Maul. This is Ethan Peterson. Sorry to call again, but I really could use your help finding some wood," I quickly blurted.

"I asked around, and there's a guy that owns a feed store on the edge of Snoqualmie that sells wood," she retorted.

She probably meant the neighboring town, but I wasn't certain. We'd been living in North Bend less than a week. "As in the next town over?"

Mrs. Maul huffed like she was annoyed at having to respond to such an inane question. And she'd been so nice when she was showing us the house…" "Of course," she replied.

"Okay, thanks. Can you tell me how to get there?"

"Take the road toward Snoqualmie, and you'll see the feed store on your left before you enter the town. Now I really must be going. Unless there's anything else?"

I got the hint that it wasn't really an offer. "Nope, thank you very much for…"

The line went dead before I finished my sentence.

****

"Firewood? Who told you I sell firewood? As you may have noticed, this is an animal feed and supply store." The bearded man with small, dark eyes behind the counter glared at me. From the moment I stepped into the small store, I felt his unfriendly gaze follow my every step toward him. He had on a thick, denim shirt under worn overalls.

I was wearing a pair of jeans and a sweater, which would be a causal outfit in San Diego, but here, my nice gray sweater and designer jeans felt very out of place. "Our landlord, or Realtor, I mean, told me that you did," I said, trying to not appear as deflated as I felt.

"Well, as you can see, there's no wood here." He waved an arm in front of him at the wares of his store.

"Yes, I can see that. Sorry to have bothered you." I nodded politely and turned toward the exit.

"I did sell some wood last year to some folks," he said when my back was turned.

I looked at him. "Oh, really?"

He smiled at me, revealing a set of less-than-perfect teeth, and it wasn't really a friendly smile. "Yup, sure did."

"Ah, okay. But not this year, huh?"

The man responded by merely shaking his head.

"Well, any chance you may know where I can find some?" I asked.

He considered my question for a moment and then responded, "I think there's a guy selling wood over in the QFC parking lot these days."

I had heard this one before. Mrs. Maul actually told us about the grocery store parking lot seller initially, too. She told us that the truck had been parked out there for weeks. However, I had driven by that parking lot every day since we had been in North Bend and had never seen a truck loaded with wood.

"I've never seen any truck there," I said.

"Musta' sold it then. Most people round here secured their wood months ago."

"Ah, well...we just moved here from California." My answer had the opposite effect I would have imagined. Instead of seeing his expression alter slightly in compassion, it turned distasteful and judging. I nodded once again and exited into a torrential downpour.

****

After getting home from work, I told Ethan that I needed some personal time. I understood that he'd tried finding firewood for us, but I was disappointed that it was taking him so long. *I mean, seriously, Ethan: How hard could it be?*

He could be defensive at times, so instead of getting into an argument, I figured the best thing for me to do was to take a long, hot bath by myself. I wanted to just grab a glass of wine, light some candles, drop in some bath salts, and be surrounded by hot water. Even though I still had a few unpacked boxes of make-up and other things stacked against a wall in my bathroom, I knew I'd find serenity in there.

The idea was also especially appealing since the house was freezing! I couldn't fathom how it could be so cold inside, when it was really not that cold outside. A temperature in the low fifties was definitely chilly, but it was not like it was in the thirties or anything.

The rain fell relentlessly for days without interruption. Earlier in the day, I'd overheard one of my coworkers talking about how it had been a record-setting downfall. I didn't really mind it too much, but a little touch of sunshine every now and again would've been welcome. I told myself that I had better get used to it.

I slipped into the inviting, steaming bathtub. The warmth of the water instantly comforted me. I took a long sip of wine; my muscles totally relaxed. I leaned my head back a little and closed my eyes for a moment.

****

In our three years together, I'd never heard Libby scream once, so her screaming from the bathroom more than startled me; it scared the hell out of me. I barreled through the boxes partially blocking the office doorway.

"Ethan!" she screamed.

Panic overtook me.

"I'm coming, Libby!" I yelled as I ran to her bathroom.

Finally, I reached her bathroom door. But I couldn't open it! There were no locks on the interior doors of the house, so I didn't understand how it could be locked. Lib kept screaming inside the bathroom, but I couldn't reach her!

"Lib! The door is locked!" I cried out. I helplessly fumbled with the doorknob.

A few moments later her, screaming stopped, and the doorknob turned. I opened the door and met with a wave of steam. Through the steam, I made out a sight I've rarely seen. Libby crying. She was seated, completely naked, on the edge of the bathtub with a distant look on her face. Water dripped from her hair around her face. I quickly grabbed a towel and wrapped it gently around her.

"Lib, what happened?" I wasn't sure she knew I'd entered the room. Her eyes stared directly forward. "Lib!"

She finally looked at me, and I saw deep fear in her eyes.

"What happened?" I asked again, sitting beside her and placing my arms around her.

"I don't know," she answered, her voice little more than a whisper. I kept my arms tight around her, waiting to see if she'd continue. "I must have fallen asleep for a second, and my head must have slipped below the water, because I woke up feeling like I was drowning."

"Oh my God, Lib. That's awful."

"Yeah, but there was something weird about it."

"I think that would be traumatic for anyone to feel."

"No, that's not what I mean," Libby said. "I heard something when my ears were under the water, just before I woke up choking."

"What was it?"

I felt Libby's small body tense and saw the goose bumps forming all over her exposed legs, even though it was still quite warm in the steamy room. "I think it was a woman's voice…saying something to me."

Libby didn't say anything more; I did my best to calm and comfort her. We figured out that her bathroom door could be locked from the inside by quickly turning the doorknob in one direction, which she must have unknowingly done. She didn't recall what the voice said to her. I chalked it up to all of the built-up stress that she's been under lately. Relocating to a new state and starting a new job all in the same week; it was a lot.

In bed, Libby snuggled against me tighter than ever. Even tighter than during the first couple of months when we got together. I held her closely too and stroked her back gently. Just as I was about to fall asleep, I heard what sounded like two mice scurrying above us.

****

I watched the internet provider's technician pull into the driveway just as I finished arranging the cabinets and cupboards with kitchen wares. I met him at the front door, noticing Mrs. Pendergrass dart off under the tall bushes in the front yard as I opened the outer screen door.

The technician looked to be about my age. He was stout, with a thick goatee. He looked friendly enough, but when I invited him into the house, he hesitated, looking around before fully stepping inside. *What was he expecting?* After a few moments, he followed me to the office, where I had my desktop computer set up. The technician gazed cautiously around the room. *Maybe he was thinking how much of a mess our house with all the boxes strewn everywhere?* Through the windows, I watched the trees swaying in the forceful wind.

"Pretty windy out there today, isn't it?" I said, trying to initiate a little small talk.

The technician, whose name I'd already forgotten, looked outside momentarily. "Yup, up here in North Bend, we get a lot more wind than other places in the area," he responded.

"Why is that?" I asked, genuinely curious.

The technician got down on his knees to begin hooking a wireless internet router and modem to my computer. "Because we're at the end of the Snoqualmie Valley and right up against the mountains," he said without turning to look at me.

"Really? I didn't know that."

The technician laughed a little. "Oh yeah. Here in North Bend, we get more wind, clouds, rain, and snow. It's also often colder here in winter, too."

I was not sure if he was mocking me or not, but it didn't matter. He was obviously a local, so I hoped I'd be able to get some good information out of him. We'd read that North Bend experienced more snow than other areas, and this was actually appealing to us after living in a place for so many years without it. But the fact that the location also meant more wind, rain, and clouds was news to me, and not really welcome news.

"Speaking of cold, do you know anywhere that we can buy some firewood for our stove?" I asked.

"You don't have any wood yet?" He looked quickly up at me in surprise.

"No, we just moved here." *Obviously, as you can see from all of the boxes around and the fact that you are hooking up our new internet connection.* "I've looked around and tried a few places, but no luck yet."

I considered telling him how I'd even called two places in response to posted signs along nearby roads and had yet to be successful. Both calls were similarly odd. For each number I'd called, I didn't receive an immediate response to my voicemail messages. At first, I'd guessed that people were less attached to their cell phones up here than back in California, or maybe that their cell reception was as crappy as mine. I'd called each number back a second time with parallel results. Then I'd begun to think that people in Western Washington had memorized California area codes and deliberately refused to answer calls from them. I'd finally reached live voices on the third call to each number.

The first guy had said that of course he'd sell us some wood, and it had sounded like a decent price. He'd said he would call me back with a time for delivery, but after I gave him my cell phone number, including the California area code, I didn't hear back.

It was pretty much the same case with the second dude. It was becoming clear that the locals distinctly hazed outsiders moving to their town. I'd expected some inherent dislike of new people moving into their small community, especially Californians, but come on, people, refusing to sell wood when you know they are going to be freezing without it?

He turned back to fiddling with some wires behind the computer. "Yeah, you really need to get some wood right quick; it's going to get really cold here soon."

It was already really cold to us.

"I think there's a place just down at the end of your street that sells wood. The family's name is Fredriksen, I believe. You could try them."

"Great, thanks. Do you know of any other places, just in case? Where do you get your wood?"

"Oh, I come from a long line of wood burners. Me and my brothers head up into the mountains every summer and get ourselves a few cords each. A lot of people around here get wood that way, or they get their wood long before now. You really need to get some soon. These little room space heaters will kill your electricity bill if you use them. And based on the size of that stove in the other room, once you get some wood in it, I'm sure it'll cook you out!"

So we've heard...

"Did you all buy this house?" he asked, shifting the conversation as he glanced a little nervously.

"No, we're just renting."

"It was for sale for a long time; I don't think any locals were interested in buying it." His voice trailed slightly, and I had the impression that he didn't mean to speak aloud all that he was thinking.

I noticed him look directly at the plastic smelly thing on the window ledge. "Why's that?" I asked.

He entirely avoided my question while he rose to his feet and changed the subject, continuing to stare at the smelly thing on the window ledge. "Y'all should check out the barbeque joint down in Truck Town sometime. I think it's the best place around." The technician stopped looking at the smelly thing and appeared to quicken his pace.

"Truck Town?"

"Yeah, that's what we locals call it. It's the next exit on the highway west of here, just another couple miles down the road. It's just a stop for truckers, the last stop, before they start heading over Snoqualmie Pass. There's just a couple of gas stations and a hotel, but one of the gas stations has a killer barbeque stand inside of it. It's not really a restaurant or anything, more like a counter and a few tables, but it's damn good food, and there's a reason all the truckers go there when they stop. Anyway, check it out sometime."

Even though he overtly avoided my question, I recognized that he was attempting to be friendly and offer a local tip as consolation. "Thanks. We'll have to check it out sometime," I responded, although Lib wasn't much of a barbeque fan, so I doubted we ever would.

"Well, that should do it. I just need to hook something up to the outside of the house, and you can walk yourself through the set up process with this disc," he said, handing me the disc. As he left I noticed him glance behind me back at the office room.

****

After I set up the internet connection, I decided to take a stroll down the street to see if I could find the place selling wood the technician mentioned—the Fredriksen's house. The name sounded Swedish to me, and I remembered reading that western Washington was originally settled by a lot of Scandinavian immigrants, and Swedes in particular.

The wind whipped around me as I walked, but it was only slightly drizzling so the walk was not so bad. Dark clouds had unfortunately totally encased the area, and I couldn't see any of the surrounding mountains that I knew were there. I couldn't even see the prominent Rattlesnake Ridge or Mount Si, which were both within a couple of miles of the house.

I figured this was at least a good opportunity to see our new neighborhood. It wasn't really so much of a neighborhood as a semi-rural road with houses on it in a pattern of nice-looking homes next to poorly maintained ones and with a few trailer homes here and there. Just down from our house was a fairly large Christmas tree lot. I also noticed how a lot of the mailboxes alongside the road were somehow propped up after their wooden posts had apparently rotted away. I wondered how long it took them to rot. Waterlogged, probably. I was already starting to feel waterlogged myself.

A huge dog suddenly charged from behind a house and aggressively barked at me on the other side of a low gate that it could surely jump over easily. *Wow, pleasant.* I ignored the barking beast as I walked on the side of the road. There was no sidewalk. I discovered a wide open area with just a couple of houses, a barn or two, and an expansive stretch of fields with a handful of horses grazing in it. One of the barns had a small gated area with what even appeared to be a couple of goats. I caught a glimpse of a lone coyote dart from the field into an area of thick brush and then noticed a bald eagle soaring high overhead. *We had sure moved a long way from San Diego.*

Suddenly, a vehicle zipped past me so close that I jumped into the tall, wet grass lining the road. I heard loud laughter coming from out of the large pick-up truck that just roared by, clearly exceeding the speed limit. I noted I should stay aware of passing cars on the road.

Many of the homes had streams of smoke emanating from their chimneys; clearly they had no problem securing winter wood stocks. A man with long hair streaking out from a baseball cap, torn jeans, and an unbuttoned flannel with a T-shirt underneath stepped out of the front door of the one of the houses. I nodded politely and said hello, but he merely gazed at me without saying a word. I noticed his T-shirt had "Pearl Jam" scrolled across the front of it.

When I reached the end of the road near where the interstate passed overhead, I found myself standing outside the property that had to be the Fredriksen's place. Thinking back, I recalled glimpsing a few huge trucks loaded with enormous piles of stripped tree trunks passing by the house occasionally; this must be where they were heading. I walked a little farther down the road to get a better view of the property and to see if there was any indication of a place for inquiries on purchasing wood.

If any such indication existed, it was well hidden. In fact, everything about the place conveyed the opposite of inviting. I was really just a city guy, so to me, it looked like one of those guarded compounds where people proclaimed that they were independent from the federal government.

First off, the property was huge and appeared to be haphazardly developed: there were at least four separate trailer homes scattered about, a few pieces of heavy machinery parked in random open spaces, various shed-like buildings interspersed around the lot, a semi-truck sitting toward the front, four or so old pick-up trucks parked near the trailer homes, and a corral with two horses grazing in it toward the rear with a small barn nearby. The trees and brush had been allowed to grow wildly, and they formed a natural barrier between the road and property. However, this had to be the place, as I could see piles of former trees in a clearing back toward the horse corral. It was unclear which of the trailers was the main one, and I would have been guessing at where to go if I tried. I also noticed a few signs posted on trees stating: "No Trespassing." *Nope, that was not the most inviting.*

These people may have indeed sold firewood, but clearly their business was conducted through long-since-established relationships with their customers, and they didn't welcome walk-ins. I imagined that I may have a better chance of being met with a shotgun pointed at me rather than a welcome greeting if I walked up to one of the trailers. I decided to abandon my effort and walk home. I wish I hadn't texted Lib about what the internet guy told me, as she was probably excited at the prospect of having a warm house. Now I'd disappoint her again. There had to be some other place to get wood.

****

It was finally Friday, and I was so happy. My first week on the new job had been challenging as any first week at a new job. Sitting on the bus from Seattle to North Bend, I tried to not notice the awful smell emanating from a man sitting five rows in front of me. My entire commute was fairly long, but I hoped I would get used to it. And since my company paid for my monthly bus pass, it was hard to turn it down. Ethan dropped me off at the bus stop and picked me up in the afternoon every day. I imagined that once he found a full-time job as well that we would have to figure out some sort of new logistical arrangement, but we'd cross that bridge when we got to it. It worked out well, and I thought it was sweet how he made coffee for me every morning.

Ethan and I had never had more than one vehicle since we'd been together; there'd never been a need, and I didn't think we could afford to have two cars anyway. All of my work colleagues kept telling me that we needed to seriously consider upgrading the one vehicle we had anyway because every winter, North Bend experienced a lot of snow, and our little Toyota wasn't going to get us through the winter. After living in San Diego for so many years, we weren't used to considering the prospect of driving in snow. Whenever we used to drive up to Big Bear for a weekend ski trip once or twice a year, getting up there had never really been that treacherous.

I just didn't know how we could possibly afford a new vehicle. My salary was nice, especially after years of low-paying, part-time administrative jobs I took to get through graduate school, but adding a monthly car payment on top of everything else would be painful.

There was Ethan, waiting diligently for me in the car at the bus stop. I noticed he was reading a book, and when he saw me, a smile extended across his face. The wind was really strong and the rain was coming down pretty hard, so I ran as best I could in the shoes I was wearing.

After I sat down in the car, I leaned over to kiss him on the cheek. "Whew…I'm glad it's Friday," I said.

"I'll bet. Congratulations on your first week at the new job," he replied.

"I could really use a relaxing evening; it's been a long week."

Ethan smiled again in response. "I thought that would be the case, so I set up the living room today and figured we could have a Friday movie night. I even picked up a pizza and some wine."

Friday movie nights with wine and pizza had been a tradition for us since we first met, and although we normally tried to eat healthy food as much as possible, I had no interest in giving up our pizza nights. Everyone should be allowed a guilty pleasure or two.

I clasped my hands in front of me and playfully giggled like a little girl. "Oh super! That sounds perfect," I responded. "Were you able to find any wood for us yet?" I asked as Ethan starting driving us home.

His expression noticeably transformed from cheery to morose, and I knew that he had blown it some way or another…

"No, unfortunately no luck yet. That place down the road was a strike out. But I picked up a box of those fake logs as well, so we'll have something to burn in the meantime."

"Those things are pricey, aren't they?"

"Yeah, they are, but it's just to get us by."

"Okay, I'm sure you'll find some wood for us soon."

"Let's hope so. You know, I noticed something weird about the house: there's no cell phone reception inside it, but if you step outdoors, it's totally fine. Odd, huh?"

"That is strange..." I admitted.

Maybe it would be chilly in the house yet again, but I was glad it was Friday all the same.

* * * *

We had encountered a small scare when we were slicing pizza in the kitchen after we made it home and Ethan started a fire with the fabricated logs of wood. We heard sharp squeaking sounds coming from somewhere in the house. At first, we thought it had to be bats in the attic, but as we honed in on where the noise was coming from, our attention was turned to beneath the kitchen sink. When Ethan opened the doors, there was no doubt where the sounds were originating. The back wall of the cupboard, which used to cover the piping connections, had totally disintegrated, and mice or rats, whichever, were clearly nearby. Maybe they were drawn to the heat of house, even if it wasn't much. I was, of course, horrified momentarily, but my capable Ethan came to the rescue. He quickly made a new wall with cardboard from our moving boxes and packing tape. Once he did, the squeaking stopped, and I felt saved from the disgusting rodents. It was pretty gross.

I took a shower and felt totally relaxed. A bath would have been nice, but after the incident earlier that week, I had decided to stay away from baths for a while. I still wasn't exactly sure what happened. I supposed that I had dozed off and choked as my head slid down below the water line; everything else was just my imagination. It must have been.

We sat down on the couch to watch television after my shower. There was a local newscast covering the subject of a rise in meth houses in outlying locations of the Seattle metropolitan area. The reporter even mentioned North Bend as being one of the specific places of concern. Having dealt with enough seriousness in my first week at work, hearing that we may be neighbors to meth labs was not at all comforting or interesting to me, and I quickly suggested that we start a movie. Ethan happily agreed and poured us a couple more glasses of wine. Even without having firewood, our Friday comfort night felt nice.

The rain then surprisingly stopped, yet there was still a ferocious wind storm. The gusts were so loud at times that we struggled to hear the movie, and we turned the volume really high. We placed a rolled up blanket at the base of the door to block the drafts of cold air that were invading our house. The store-bought logs didn't do more than slightly warm the little fireplace room alone next to the living room, and we were covered in blankets. Still, it was kind of romantic being there snuggled next to my husband. I suggested to Ethan that we step outside onto our tiny covered front doorway to catch some of nature's display occurring all around us. He agreed, and we paused the movie.

The fierce wind slammed the outer screen door behind us as soon as we stepped outside on to the concrete steps. There was so much noise from the gusts blowing through every tree and bush that it sounded like freight trains passing from all directions.

I momentarily felt a surge of panic as I remembered that the front door had an old handle that automatically locked once the door was closed and was worried that it may get blown shut as well. I looked back at the door, and Ethan opened his palm, showing the key. I sighed in relief.

Huge branches fell all around and on the house. Suddenly, we realized that it may not have been entirely safe to stand outside. We returned inside to the slight warmth of the house. Before long, I found myself nodding off on the couch. I didn't even make it to the end of the movie.

* * * *

We spent the day after the wind storm unpacking. I also picked up all of the fallen branches that were scattered throughout our yard and driveway. Some of the branches were huge, and by the end of my effort, I had a large pile accumulated in the back corner of the yard. It would have been great if I could have chopped them for firewood, but the wood was too wet anyway.

The day turned out to be free of rain and partly cloudy. Occasionally, the sun would sneak through an opening in the clouds and tease us with its presence. I'd learned a charming expression people used in the Pacific Northwest to describe this: sun breaks.

We were just getting ready to drive over to see the famed Snoqualmie Falls, but as we were getting into the car, we discovered that overnight, someone spray painted something on the rear window of our car. Probably, it had happened after the rain stopped, which was creepy to think there had been someone sneaking around our house in the middle of the night—perhaps even while we were even still watching a movie inside. Lib wanted to call the sheriff's office right away. Both of our moods dropped after seeing it, so the falls would have to wait for another day. The blue paint spelled: GO HOME.

    This certainly was a lovely welcome to the neighborhood.

Chapter 2

November

My initial impression of the sheriff was of an old school, no bull shit type. He stepped out of his police cruiser wearing a wide brimmed hat, aviator sunglasses, pressed blue uniform, and polished black boots; his mustache was thick but perfectly trimmed. He looked around the property before acknowledging me at the front door.

Eventually, he turned toward me. "Howdy," he said.

I'd heard that expression often since we'd moved, though I thought it was reserved for more "western" states like Montana or Wyoming.

"You called for me," he stated. I instantly had the impression that he felt his time was being wasted. He avoided looking at me directly and spit off to the side.

"Hello, Sheriff. Thank you for coming over," I responded as politely as I could.

I couldn't see his eyes beneath his large sunglasses, but I felt him glaring at me, waiting for me to continue. I stepped down from our doorway and walked toward our car. "Yesterday morning, we called about this," I said as I pointed to the back of the car where the blue "GO HOME" was still bright, even in the cloudy, dark morning light.

When we called, we were told that the sheriff wouldn't be able to make it over to our house until today. True, our graffiti was no emergency. Fair enough. But I wondered what had kept him busy enough to delay him an entire day. I didn't imagine there were too many high emergency days in North Bend.

The sheriff ambled toward the back of our car and glanced at the graffiti, then back over to the house. The first thing he said was, "Huh, guess you'll want to get your license plate changed from California to Washington." His tone was entirely unsympathetic.

"Yeah, I was planning on registering the car soon; just haven't gotten to it yet with all of the other things we've had to do since moving here."

He turned to gaze at the house. "So you just moved in here?"

"Yes, just recently."

The sheriff's stare remained fixed on the house a few moments longer before he pivoted back to the car. "How do you like living in this house?"

It was an odd and unexpected question. "Uh, fine so far."

He didn't look at me and just kept starting at the house, and I had the impression that he was familiar with it somehow. After so long, I interrupted. "Everything's good except people spray painting the back of our car, that is," I said.

My words broke his apparent trance. "Well, some people 'round here aren't too happy with all of the city people moving out here," he replied.

I thought how unfair he was to automatically label us "city people" when we'd relocated from out of state. "We thought we should let you know in case there were other occurrences in the neighborhood recently," I said.

The sheriff shook his head. "Nope, just here," he offered.

We both stood in silence for a long moment, staring at the back of the car. Of course, it began to sprinkle.

"There are products you can buy at the hardware store that help to remove paint from glass. I'll have to file a brief report on this since you called to have me come out here. And that's about all that can be done," he concluded, walking to his cruiser.

I was still standing behind our car, questioning if I was dreaming or not. "Thank you for coming over," I managed to say. *Yeah, thanks a lot for coming over for nothing, Sheriff Jackass*, I thought.

The sheriff responded by slightly waving a hand before getting into his cruiser and driving away. So apparently we wouldn't be able to rely on the authorities to be of much help if anything else happened.

A thought occurred to me that I tried to hide: Maybe we should have stayed in California. I decided that when I retold this story to Libby later, I'd leave out how unfriendly the sheriff had been.

*****

Finally, *finally*, I'd found a place to buy firewood. I couldn't believe such a simple thing had been so difficult; regardless, it had finally happened. Driving around town again after the sheriff's visit, I saw a sign stating firewood for sale with a phone number. I called the number once, but when I got the answering machine, I didn't leave a message, not daring to leave a California number on an answering machine again. I kept calling every half hour for two hours until someone picked up. When I did get a live person on the phone, it sounded like an older lady, and she briskly informed me that I needed to speak to her husband, Butch, and gave me his cell phone number. I tried confirming that I had jotted down the correct number, but she hung up before I could ask.

Butch answered his phone right away and told me all that all he had left in his stock was fir for two hundred and fifty dollars a cord. I'd heard that fir wasn't the best wood to use. It supposedly burned quickly, but I couldn't have cared less: we needed firewood for our freezing little house. Lib was freezing whenever she was home, and it seemed to be leading to a chilling of her attitude, as well.

The internet technician had mentioned that this time of year, one should expect to pay two hundred per cord due to the lateness in the season and that normal pricing in the late summer months was around one hundred fifty a cord.

Butch said that he'd be over within an hour to drop off the wood, and he pointedly stated that he only accepted cash payments. I asked if perhaps it would be better to wait until it wasn't raining to deliver the wood, due to the light but steady rain. Butch assured me that a little rain wouldn't do any harm to the wood as long as it didn't sit in it too long. He added that if he waited for it to stop raining, he wouldn't be able to deliver it until July.

Point taken. While I waited, I wondered how much wood was in a cord.

My question of how much wood made up a cord was answered when a giant truck pulled to a stop in front of the house with logs filling its large cargo hold. The previous light rain had turned into a steady barrage, and the wood wasn't covered. That couldn't be good for anything meant to be burned, no matter what Butch had said.

When Butch rolled down his window, I got my first glimpse of him as I walked out to his truck. He was an older man, wearing a stained ball cap. He had an unshaven face and a few missing teeth. A middle-aged woman with stringy hair sitting next to him took a gulp of Mountain Dew. He introduced himself and his daughter and asked where I wanted the wood dumped. I told him in the driveway near the back of the house where I'd pile it would be fine. The daughter jumped out of the truck and guided him as he backed into our driveway. The back of the truck then slowly lifted up, and the split logs of wood crashed loudly onto the ground. It was about twenty yards to the place under the back porch's awning where I planned to stack the wood. Clearly, I'd be busy for the next few hours.

Butch smiled greedily when I handed him the cash. "Hell, if you'd given me the cash first, I would've just kept my wood."

I didn't find the joke funny.

His daughter then mentioned that she'd be willing to stack the wood for a hundred dollars. I wasn't sure if she was joking or not as well, but I politely declined.

Before they pulled away, Butch rolled down his window. "I reckon you'll burn through at least a couple of cords over the season. If you want any more, give me a call," he said to me as I stood in the rain. "Bet it's cold in there," he added. He peered around me, trying to look in through one of the front windows.

"Any chance you'd give us a discount if we do?"

Butch grinned in response and shook his head.

As I carried and stacked the wood, various thoughts swirled in my head. One was that a cord was a hell of a lot of wood, and I couldn't imagine us burning through it in a season. Another was that even though I was definitely no expert, a lot of the pieces of wood felt overly heavy, almost waterlogged. And it had also been strange how Butch made the comment on his assumption that it was cold in our house and then the way he looked at the front windows. But at least Lib would be happy that I finally was able to get us some wood.

* * * *

I realized that he tried, but sometimes, I got so frustrated with Ethan. I kept telling him that he needed to start the fire in the stove earlier in the afternoons. He must have been starting it late, likely right before he picked me up from the bus stop after work because it was not at all warm when we arrived home. Ethan worried about money often, so I knew he was trying to conserve our wood supply as much as possible. But thanks to him, we hadn't felt the house get warm even after hours of burning wood. I was so frustrated with him.

And honestly, I just didn't understand why the house was so cold. Had the insulation been installed at the same time the house was built nearly a hundred years ago or something? It sure seemed like it. Even when Ethan did get a good, solid fire going for a few hours before we went to sleep, I would wake up in the middle of the night with the air in the house so cold, it felt like we were sleeping outside.

And I still didn't understand why certain areas of the house smelled so bad. I tried to ignore it because I knew I had a crazy keen sense of smell, but whatever that odor was, it didn't seem to go away. I couldn't quite describe the smell; it was like no stench I'd ever noticed before, but whatever it was, it was strong and foul. And Ethan's "office" was the worst. *How could he stand to sit in there?*

We decided to sneak in a little walk before dinner. It was dark, and Ethan carried a flashlight. There was a break in the rain, and I was glad to be getting a little exercise. Although, it was really chilly outside.

After less than a quarter mile down the road, I asked, "Ethan, does it feel a little relieving to you, as well, being out of the house together?"

"Yeah, I guess a little, now that you mention it," he responded. "What makes you ask?"

"Oh, I don't know. Just something I noticed. It sure feels colder than it really is, doesn't it?"

"Yeah. I think the general dampness makes it feel colder," Ethan replied.

I was frankly surprised by how cold I felt most of the time. The temperature wasn't even that low; well, of course compared to Southern California, it was low, but compared to most places, it was not that cold. But I thought Ethan had a point that there was something about the moisture surrounding everything combined with the lack of sun that was perpetually chilling.

"How's the job going?" Ethan asked.

"It's fine. I'm still getting used to the company and my coworkers, but I'm busy and interested in what I'm doing."

"That's good."

"Have you started looking for a new job yet?" I asked. The plan had always been for Ethan to handle the moving-in details and continue his part-time job, then to apply for positions as soon as we were settled. I really hoped he wasn't flaking out on trying already.

"No, I haven't yet. I still need to get the car registered, move our bank accounts, get a new cell phone with a local number, and get all of those changes of address done. In between, I've been picking up some hours here and there for work. I figure I'll be set in a couple of weeks to really jump into it."

I felt the urge to mention that he should at least start looking for jobs. In the current economy, it could be a while before he even landed an interview, but I held off. "Are you getting more used to making the fire?" I asked.

"Yeah, I think so. I think the wood that the old jerk sold us is a little wet. It's really difficult to get the fire started and then keep it going. And I've burned my hands a few times already."

I'd noticed the burns on his hands, and they looked painful. "You should start wearing gloves."

"Yeah, I should."

"Maybe it'll get easier as you get more used to working with the stove and the wood will dry a little now that it's under the awning."

"Hopefully."

As Ethan replied, the temporary reprieve in rain abruptly ended and a heavy deluge pounded down on us and everything in North Bend. Luckily, we were not too far from the house, and we ran down the street, as we hadn't brought an umbrella. We ran up to the house to shelter ourselves under the front door's small porch. We were both drenched and freezing, but it had been kind of fun, and we both smiled like kids. Ethan reached into his pocket to get his set of keys, and it took him a few seconds to find the key hole since it was so dark.

It occurred to me that we had left the light above the front door purposefully on when we left. "Didn't we leave the front light on?" I asked. We both hurried to get inside, which unfortunately wasn't all that much warmer.

"Yeah, that's right, we did," Ethan confirmed.

We both turned to look at the light switch near the door and saw that it was definitely flipped upwards. Ethan tested it by flicking it up and down a few times, with no change resulting on the porch.

"Must just be an old light bulb we need to replace," I commented.

Ethan shook his head in disagreement. "Nope, I actually replaced it with a new eco-efficient bulb just yesterday." There was a moment of silence between us before Ethan said, "Must have been a bad bulb. I'll replace it tomorrow."

****

I was down to the last room left to unpack and arrange, the room that Mrs. Maul had called the sun room; I was getting really tired of organizing the house. I could see why one would call it a sun room, as two of its walls were primarily comprised of picture windows, but we definitely hadn't seen much sunshine that would justify the title for the small space. It was pretty cool, though, as it looked out toward the backyard and open fields beyond with a great view of Rattlesnake Ridge on the horizon. Of course, we only were able to enjoy the view when the ridgeline was not obscured by clouds. So far, my only name for it was the "cold room." The insulation out there was even worse than the rest of the house, and as soon as I got the room set up, I was going to figure out a way to temporarily block it off. I hoped it would help with heating the house.

There was something weird setting on the sideboard in the corner—some sort of light brown object. I wiggled around a pile of boxes to get over there and see what it was. After I picked it up, I still didn't recognize it. It looked and felt like a jagged piece of ceramic pottery that was broken off something else, but I couldn't imagine what that could have been. I knew that Lib hadn't been in this room since I'd moved in the sideboard, the dining table, and a stack of boxes. She actually refused to step into the room, as it was so much colder than the rest of the house. *So how in the hell did this thing get here?*

I had never seen it before, nor had I seen whatever it must have broken off of in the first place, and I certainly hadn't placed it on the sideboard. I hadn't hung anything on the walls in the room yet that it could have broken from, and the stack of boxes was on the other side of the room. That ruled out any possibility that something I was unaware of broke in the move and somehow miraculously ended up here. I felt a slight chill move through me as I peered around the room. Of course, no one else had been here.

I carefully examined the piece of pottery, if that's what it was. It had a faded smudge of something reddish on it. I ran my thumb over it and felt an eerie twinge of discomfort as it flaked the way dried blood would.

Rain poured down once again.

* * * *

Who knows what that pottery shard thing I found in the sun room was, but I decided to not tell Libby about it; it would only freak her out. I was a little freaked out about it myself, but there must have been an explanation. I tossed the thing in the garbage and told myself to forget about it. I also replaced the front porch light bulb, and it worked fine.

I finally had the house all unpacked and set up and a wood supply secured, so I could start putting in some work hours with a clear head. I still had various other relocation tasks to do, but I planned on intermingling a little of each of those over the following couple of weeks. My boss down in San Diego was probably getting a little anxious that I hadn't signed on for assignments yet.

My work deal was that I was a contributing editor for a blog related to green building and sustainable development issues. "Contributing Editor" may have been a bit of a stretch. Really, I was just the lowest member of my group, and I was more of a research assistant who provided background on assigned topics. Other people wrote the articles and took all the credit. Someday, I would be like one of them, though. I knew it.

Lib didn't like me doing it, because she thought my boss paid me too little for the amount of work I put into each assignment. But I was pleased to have some sort of income available while I looked for something more permanent. It may not have been much, but it was something. And these were areas that interested me both personally and professionally, so I took pride in my work, even if I didn't receive much credit for my efforts.

I planned to start looking for a new job, but I really despised job searching so didn't feel motivated to jump into it. I thought I'd be better off getting in as many hours at my existing job as I could, regardless of what Libby thought. After all, I was the one doing all of the relocation stuff, and it was a pain in the ass by itself.

It was time to put the headphones on and get to work...

* * * *

What was that? Even with my headphones on, I swore I heard a loud bang from somewhere inside the house. It sounded like it was in the room on the other side of the office wall, which was a weird little room in between the main bedroom and the wood burning stove room, near Libby's bathroom.

I took off my headphones and waited to hear it again. A few minutes passed without anything. I slowly walked into the other rooms of the house, thinking that perhaps something had just fallen over, but everything looked fine. The noise must have come from outside, I reassured myself.

When I stepped back into my office room, I noticed a few flies on the picture frame I kept on my desk of Libby and I. Flies in November? I shooed them off and planned to chase them through the house to kill them. But after they flew out of the room, I couldn't find them again, and I searched every other room, every other window.

After giving up on the hunt, I sat down at my desk and resumed working. A thought occurred to me that when I was searching for the flies, the bedroom door had been slightly opened, and I was fairly certain I had closed it before I'd left to drop Lib off at the bus stop. Maybe I had not, though.

Just as I began reading a very long email from my boss, I noticed Mrs. Pendergrass was outside in the yard, hopping around. It made me smile when I saw her out there, if she was indeed a "her." The day before, there had also been a couple of deer in the front yard, outside my office. As soon as I moved to grab a camera, they noticed me and darted away. I was a bit surprised they were so skittish at the sight of a person when they had no qualms about walking through yards.

After I did a little work, I thought I'd head down to Issaquah to pick up some house plants for us. I'd always liked having plants around; it just made a place feel more alive.

*****

"Oh my God...Ethan, have you smelled inside some of these cupboard drawers in here?" I asked from the kitchen. Ethan was struggling to keep the fire burning again in the next room.

"What do you mean?" he called back. I heard him yelp in pain slightly, and I was sure he'd burned one of his hands on the stove yet again.

"I mean some of these lower drawers totally smell like mold," I added.

"Really? That's probably no good, then?" he offered.

"Um, yeah, Ethan. It's no good. Didn't you notice it when you were putting stuff in here?"

Ethan appeared in the doorway between the kitchen and the stove room. "No, I didn't, Lib. But I wasn't really taking time to smell everywhere when I was trying to unpack."

I heard a slight annoyance in his tone. We rarely got into arguments, but there were times when we could get on each other's nerves for sure. This was one of those times.

I held back from what I really wanted to say, which was that he needed to pay more attention at times. "Okay, well, we shouldn't use any of these drawers down here, though, or our stuff is going to get ruined." I emptied the drawers, and Ethan returned to fiddling with the fire. I heard him curse and imagined he'd burned his hand once again. *God, when did he turn into such a klutz?*

I wanted to ask him again how his job search was going, as it had been a few weeks by then, but I was sure he would just tell me that he hadn't really had time to look. He would say that between getting us settled and keeping up his hours with the blog company, he'd been too occupied. This may have been true, but I believed it would be better for him to get a full-time job. I decided to hold off on pressuring him too much since I knew he stressed out easily. But the mold thing still ticked me off. It was such an overpowering smell. How could he have possibly missed it?

* * * *

When we woke up the next day, I suggested that we get out of the house for a little while. Even though we'd averted a spat, I had felt tension between us the entire evening. Maybe what we really needed was some fresh air. It would have been nice to do a little hike, but it was another gloomy day outside, with clouds, wind, and rain. Hiking in the rain just didn't sound enjoyable.

The weather seemed worse in North Bend compared to westward toward Seattle. Many days while riding the bus back from work, I observed a very noticeable difference toward North Bend. Most days, no matter how cloudy or rainy it was in Seattle, it looked even cloudier and darker to the east in the direction of our house. I came up with a new name that I shared with Ethan that made him laugh: "North Cloud." Even though it was kind of funny, it did strike me that we had decided to live in such a dark place.

Miserable weather conditions or not, I suggested that we drive to see Snoqualmie Falls, as apparently it was a big deal, according to people in my office. We hadn't made it there yet after our last attempt was ruined by the punks who'd vandalized our car.

Then we could stop at Twede's Cafe downtown, although it was not really much of a "downtown." Someone at work told me how the diner was famous for having been featured regularly on the television series *Twin Peaks*. All I really remembered about that show was that it was super weird and dark. There was a girl's unexplained murder, a midget speaking some bizarre language, incest, and a lot of overall unclear crazy stuff going on. Weird and dark sure seemed to about the right fit for this place.

As I walked out of the bedroom, I noticed the outline of footprints on the hardwood floor in the living room and stove room. We had agreed not to wear shoes inside the house. I considered that they could have been from when he was moving in boxes, and I just never noticed. Maybe it was that the light. What little light there was hit the footprints perfectly to reveal them. I grabbed some paper towels, wetted them slightly in the sink, and wiped away the footprints. The footprints looked though like they were from some sort of boots, and I couldn't picture which of Ethan's shoes could have left such prints.

* * * *

The waterfall was impressive, I had to admit. Even in the chilly weather and sprinkling rain, it was impossible to not recognize the beauty of the place. There was a massive amount of water funneling over a ledge and falling what looked like a few hundred feet. As we got nearer to the overlook, our faces were covered in a mist that spewed outward from the falls, and although it was cold, I almost felt refreshed by it. Ethan held me close and kissed me right there, water dripping from the ends of our noses.

A large, regal-looking building was perched on the edge of the falls above us.

"That building is actually an old hotel that they converted into an upscale resort and spa," Ethan told me as we started walking back to our car.

"How do you know that?" I asked.

"Oh, you know, I've read some about the history of the region. You know how I like to get to know areas."

"Yes, I do, and I think it's cute." I clung to his arm as we crossed the bridge leading to the parking area.

Should I mention something to him about the other night, the tension mounting between us? I'd been worried about its escalation. *No, I shouldn't ruin the moment.* I just loved not feeling any tension between us.

After our visit to the falls, we headed back to North Bend for brunch, passing through the cute town of Snoqualmie on the way, which we had gone around on the way there. Ethan pointed out the signs indicating the town's history tied to logging and the railroad. This historical background was clearly displayed with some sort of railway exhibit and an enormous tree section that had been cut and set right alongside the road.

After we passed through the downtown area, we saw an "elk crossing" road sign and both agreed that we'd never seen one of those before. Then when we got closer to North Bend, we passed by a huge elk casually crossing the road in between traffic. It reminded me of the opening sequence for that old show *Northern Exposure*.

At Twede's, we each ordered equally sounding gluttonous meals that included scrambled eggs, potatoes, cheese, meat, and vegetables covered in a white, thick gravy—the perfect comfort food for a cold and gloomy day.

The diner was nothing too special and, if anything, seemed a bit rundown. I would have thought that such a supposed "institution" would be better maintained. The booth seats we sat in were ill-formed and uncomfortable after decades of abuse, no doubt the work of too many fat asses pummeling them. The chipped veneer of the table was visible at the corners.

The most endearing quality of the place was the funky wall hangings around the place and then a wall across from the restrooms covered with photos from the *Twin Peaks* set. We asked our waitress, an overweight girl with too much dark eye makeup and a hideous lip piercing, the origin of the name of the series. She told us that one side of Mount Si had two peaks that inspired the name for the series.

While waiting for our food, Ethan commented on how many people were decked out in Seattle Seahawks football gear. We also both agreed, in hushed voices, that from what we'd seen, it appeared that North Bend definitely was a distinct mix of a little rough, perhaps a bit *rednecky*, true local presence, and wealthy people living on its outskirts in secluded, beautiful areas, who were relative newcomers to the area and had moved outward from Seattle and its western suburbs. And there was not a lot in between. While we had expected some of both, we had not expected to find such an extremity.

"You know what I think is probably the greatest thing about living up here?" Ethan then asked.

I couldn't imagine what he was going to come up with, and I wanted to hear his opinion.

"Cheap seafood...and not just fish, but shellfish, as well. It's seriously like half the price than it was in California," he remarked. I had noticed how he made some sort of seafood dish for dinner for us at least twice a week.

There was a couple sitting at a booth next to us that seemed very interested in our conversation. The man kept staring at me, and the woman leaned back in her seat at times to better overhear us.

In Spanish, I mentioned someone was staring. It was a trick we sometimes used for privacy, but one that didn't always work in California, since more people were bilingual.

Ethan responded in Spanish, too, telling me that he believed it to be a cultural difference for people to stare more than in other places.

He said he was often surprised by how often people stared at him when he was grocery shopping.

We laughed after Ethan added that perhaps the biggest difference was that in California, everyone was too preoccupied with themselves to notice anyone else. It was fun chatting in another language. We hadn't done it since we had moved.

"I've noticed a couple of things while walking to and from the bus stop in downtown Seattle, as well," I offered.

"Like what?"

"A lot of people dress like they are about to go hiking or camping more so than heading into work. And I've never seen so many young guys with beards," I replied.

Ethan stroked his chin reflectively. "Maybe I should grow a beard?"

I reached across the table and smacked his arm lightly. "No! You know I don't like beards."

The couple in the booth next to us stopped paying attention to us once we began speaking in Spanish. I saw them talking to each other, but they were not talking loud enough for me to hear them. When they got up to leave, the man, who was wearing a plaid flannel shirt and think canvas work pants, stopped next to our booth.

"You the folks that moved into that little yellow house over on Maloney Grove?" he asked us. His tone was more curious than polite.

"Yeah, we are. I'm Ethan, and this is my wife, Libby. Are you one of our neighbors?" Ethan asked.

The man scratched a little at his unkempt beard before responding. "Nope," he eventually replied.

"Then how did you know we live there?" I asked.

"Seen your car. California plate, right? I live down the road from you," he replied. "Y'all got any kids?"

"No," I responded.

The woman stood at the entrance of the restaurant, casting him an annoyed glance. As he began to leave, he turned back and said to us, "Good luck with it."

We thanked him without really knowing why. The man and woman spoke to one another and glanced back at us. I tried to listen to what they were saying, and I saw that Ethan was trying to, as well.

When they left, I asked Ethan, "Did you hear what they were talking about?"

"I couldn't really understand, but sounded like they said something about *murder*." Ethan shook his head. "Just another couple of crazies from up here, I guess." He added, "*Extraño.*"

I smiled and agreed. It was weird.

When our plates were set before us, we looked at each other and burst into laughter, not letting the odd encounter with the guy get to us. Both of us had hearty appetites, but these plates were gigantic! There was honestly enough food on our plates for the two of us to share breakfast, lunch, and dinner…for a couple of days.

We dove in all the same, trying to hold back our snickering. Ten minutes later, with barely a dent in our respective heaping piles of delicious, artery-clogging food, we admitted defeat.

"Let's be sure to go for a walk later this afternoon to work off some of these calories," I pleaded as left the restaurant.

* * * *

Despite the fact that Ethan started the fire as soon as we returned from our excursion, it was still freezing by the time we climbed into bed. How that was even possible, I had no idea. Maybe Ethan had the flute thing or whatever it was called in the stove turned the wrong way. Regardless, I wondered how anyone could have ever lived in this house.

I heard what must have been a mouse scurry in the wall behind our heads. I knew Ethan heard it as well, but neither of us said anything. Like me, he was probably hoping the noise would not keep us from falling asleep It was raining harder outside, and the steady pounding on the roof above us would drown out all other noise before long.

We had watched a news segment earlier on the television that was a little unsettling and, lying there trying to fall asleep with something moving around above us, remembering it disturbed me. The reporter stated how this November had set numerous records, including being the coldest on record, having received more rainfall in the month than any previous November, having had subsequent days of getting more rainfall in a day than ever recorded, et cetera. And it wasn't even Thanksgiving yet!

The wind picked up on top of the rain. Something crashed loudly against the roof, and it startled me for a moment. It must have been a large branch from one of the trees around the house.

Chapter 3

December

Thanksgiving came and went, and with it also came a reportedly unprecedented snow storm. We endured about two feet of snow during the storm that lasted a few days. Weather forecasters stated that in the entire Puget Sound region, North Bend received more snow than anywhere else. Of course, at first, Libby and I loved the arrival of snow, as for us, it was something different. But with snow, there were also fierce, howling winds that swept through the Snoqualmie Valley and focused their force directly at North Bend. The cold air snuck into the house from all around us, and it was impossible to locate where the drafts were originating. And then, with limbs heavy with wet snow, the winds started breaking them off the trees like twigs, and power lines went down, knocking out our electricity for a few days.

The situation was fun at first to walk around in blankets, light candles, and cook on the wood burning stove, but the situation quickly went from amusing to miserable. We ran out of hot water on the first day and on the second had to move everything from our refrigerator and freezer into a cooler we buried outside in the snow. Keeping the fire going was especially daunting, and I could hear the wind whipping down the chimney every time I opened the stove's door. It was not fun.

We hadn't planned to visit our families for Thanksgiving, as we didn't have extra money to pay for the tickets and both of our sets of parents lived on the other side of the country: mine in Missouri and Lib's in North Carolina. Though we had planned to make our own traditional Thanksgiving dinner on our own. It would have to wait.

The storm was also a rude awakening that our little car wasn't going to work, especially if it was going to be as harsh of a winter as had been predicted. Libby had to stay home from work an extra day because we couldn't even get out of the driveway. Under the circumstances, I was sure she would have preferred to have been at work. I would have preferred to be anywhere else, too, after the second day. At least at work in an office, it would have been warm. Spending a day at home in a cold house with no electricity was far less romantic than it sounded. And we weren't even encouraged to wander outside into the snow, since it was dark with a heavy, thick cloud cover. Daylight began to diminish at three o'clock in the afternoon, and the punishing wind never ceased.

When December arrived and the snow began to melt as the precipitation switched back to rain, we began shopping for a new car. Maybe if we had been the stay-at-home type all the time on the weekends, we would have been able to get through the winter okay, but the whole reason we had decided to move to North Bend instead of closer to the city was because we wanted to get into the mountains and travel into the surrounding region as much as possible.

We had even started planning for it before we moved when we put money aside in order to buy season passes to go skiing at the resort at the pass just up Interstate 90. Neither of us were superb skiers, by any means, but we both loved it and wanted to get more into it now that it was a much more accessible activity for us. And the resort recently opened after the Thanksgiving storm.

We spent a Saturday driving to different dealerships looking for a new car, hoping to find a good deal on a used all-wheel drive vehicle.

I didn't know what it was, but car salesmen always bothered me. Even if they were pleasant, I never trusted them.

We ended up buying a used small SUV that I wasn't sure we could afford, considering the monthly payments to come, but Libby thought once I found a full-time job, it would be fine. It was a tough job market, but eventually, something had to work out for me. I had some money still saved to contribute what I could toward our expenses, but it was definitely time for me to start getting serious about the job search thing.

The hour or so drive home was fun, and I liked driving our new vehicle. Having spent my adult life driving a car, sitting higher up in a SUV was totally different. Lib and I talked about how we could drive our new tougher vehicle up into the Cascades to go skiing soon.

When we turned onto our road, Libby said, "I hope the pigeons don't poo all over our new vehicle."

Her comment made me laugh. "You said 'poo'..." After we shared a laugh, I added that I very much agreed with her. Pigeons often perched on the telephone lines next to the house.

But when we pulled into the driveway and I looked up to their usual perch, I didn't see any pigeons; they had been replaced by three crows. The big black birds squawked loudly at us. It felt like they were watching us.

After the nice ride home together, it was quite unexpected when moments later, we were on the verge of an argument as I grew frustrated trying to get a fire going.

"Why is it still so difficult for you to start a fire after you've been doing it every day for what, over month now?" she asked, obviously annoyed. She didn't stop there. "Ethan, I'm so tired of the house being so damned cold!"

"I know, I know. As you can clearly see, I'm trying."

"Well, try harder!"

I bit my tongue. But as she passed me at the stove on her way to the kitchen, she added a comment on how one of the house plants that I got for us was obviously dead and another looked as if it would be soon.

I went on the defensive. "Yes, I know. I can see that very well. But I don't know what the hell else to do! You know that I've always taken good care of our houseplants, but for some reason, it's different with these, and these are even the hardiest plants I could find!" I turned away from her general direction, hoping to avoid further judgment of my apparent shortcomings.

Libby muttered something to herself in the kitchen just loud enough for me to hear about me not trying hard enough for many things. I decided to do us both a favor and ignored her, keeping quiet for the remainder of the evening.

* * * *

There was yet another unsettling noise. We knew we had mice in the walls of the house, and we suspected there were bats in the attic, as well. Then the neighborhood cats for some reason picked our house as a congregation point in the middle of the night.

Lucky Ethan appeared to sleep right through it, but I clearly heard at least two cats doing that low growl thing that cats did, and it sounded like they were inside the house! I didn't know how that could be possible. It was 3:33 a.m., and my mind was not exactly functioning clearly, but it did sound like they were right next to us. They must have been just outside of the house, just beyond our bedroom wall. Then again, maybe they had figured out how to get into the space underneath the house? Wherever they were, it was so annoying and such an unpleasant way to be woken up, I doubted I was going to be able to fall asleep again. *How could Ethan sleep through all that screeching?*

I felt hot and sweaty, and not in a good way. It was like waking up with a fever, but I wasn't sick. I was annoyed and exhausted, though, and I was not looking forward to going to work in the morning.

Arriving home to North Cloud after work, I was completely exhausted. Ethan said he hadn't heard the cats. I honestly found that hard to believe. In fact, it annoyed me thinking he pretended he didn't hear them. I was also annoyed by the cold and wind and rain, which never stopped. The snow from the November storm had melted into slushy patches, resulting in my shoes being wet all the time.

When we got home, the house was freezing. Ethan claimed he had started the fire hours before. I thought he was lying, but I didn't say anything. He claimed that he had worked all afternoon on research for a blog article, too, but I pictured that he spent most of the time playing on Facebook or something. *What a terrific use of his time.*

I quickly went to the bedroom to get away from him. Ethan had for some reason closed the bedroom door again. I wanted the bedroom to get some of the heat from the fire, even if it was minimal. He knew that. Without it, I felt like we were sleeping in a freezer. I called out to Ethan, who'd returned to his room, where he spent almost all of his time. I asked him why he'd closed the bedroom door. He answered something about having purposefully left it open earlier in the day…*yeah, right.*

I wasn't going to pursue it any further. Obviously, he had a reason to leave the door closed, and he didn't want to explain it to me. But why couldn't he just tell me instead of ignoring me?

Even if it was colder in the bedroom, especially thanks to my dumb-at-times husband closing the door, of all the rooms in the house, I liked it most. Despite the horrible cat and mice noises. After lying on the bed, doing nothing for a while, I then retreated to a hot shower. I felt better as the water pounded against my body. It felt so good, I actually got goose bumps. The tantalizing sensation reminded me how much the passion between Ethan and I had dwindled since moving.

I turned off the shower and stood for a few moments with a towel wrapped around my body, enjoying the brief feeling of warmth.

Then I heard something move in the wall next to me! My moment of pleasure instantly transformed into shock.

"Ethan!" I screamed.

He opened the bathroom door and peered through the thick steam. "Are you okay?"

I pointed to the wall behind the showerhead as I quickly stepped from the shower basin. "There's something alive in the wall!"

Ethan came farther into the bathroom and put his ear against the wall. After a few seconds, he said, "I don't hear anything, Lib. Maybe it was just the pipes settling after you turned off the water; it is an old house, after all."

I didn't like his tone; I didn't like it at all. "It's not the fucking pipes. I heard something moving in there!"

Neither of us dropped "F-bombs" too often, so I knew Ethan recognized that I was not joking. He turned and held me close to him. "I'm sorry, Lib; I believe you. Tomorrow, I'll see if I can borrow a ladder from a neighbor and look up in the attic to see if I can see anything up there that may be getting down into the walls."

I felt momentarily consoled by him and appreciated his offer.

I felt even more understood when at 3:33 a.m. that night I felt him stir and awaken in bed next to me. He also heard the apparent feline orgy being held somewhere just outside of our cold bedroom.

* * * *

It had been a long week, and I wasn't getting much accomplished. I had only received one research assignment for work, and the job search, which I had begun to get into more earnestly, had been generally dismal. I'd submitted thirty applications and hadn't even gotten a call back. *Was there anything more humiliating than job searching when you really need to find one?*

I had also begun to notice that whenever I left the office, which I started to refer to as "my room," I felt myself being pulled back to it. For some reason, I felt more comfortable in that room than anywhere else in the house. Like I didn't want to be anywhere else.

I decided I would ask a neighbor to borrow a ladder to see what was in attic beyond the secret window at the front of the house. I didn't really have anything else better to do.

Then something kind of strange happened when I was getting ready to head outside. I closed my room's door, and when I stepped into the living room, I felt this overwhelming force of something pushing against me.

And then closing the door itself, I sensed some kind of resistance, like the door didn't want to be shut. I wondered if I was just imagining it because I didn't really want to go outside in the cold, away from the sanctuary of my room. It was a day that one would rather stay inside, and definitely not one to be perched outside on a ladder, after all. But as the perceived force or whatever I was most likely imagining began to dissipate, I dismissed it as drafts blowing through the house and focused on my task to find a ladder.

The house directly across from ours constantly had its blinds drawn, and the only sign of life I ever noticed was that at times, the giant pick-up truck in its driveway was gone. The house to the left sat across a long stretch of an unmaintained property, and it looked like what I pictured as the stereotypical image of a meth house. Blinds always covered the windows. Trash was strewn all around, the light at the front of the house had broken off from its fixture and dangled by a cord, and there were two rusting cars parked next to one another on the side of the road. On top of that, I'd noticed cars frequently coming and going from the house during the day—different cars—and whoever lived there let their two ferocious looking dogs, which must have had some pit bull in them, run loose outside.

But I supposed if they were doing us no harm, there was no need to concern myself with them. That's how it was in California anyway. I picked the house with the closed blinds and the giant pick-up truck. I thought they were my best bet.

I knocked on the door. A woman in a faded red, cotton bathrobe, holding a cigarette, opened the door and eyed me suspiciously. "You selling sometin'?" she asked before I had a chance to say hello.

"Oh no, no…I'm your neighbor actually. My wife and I moved into the house next door a few months back," I responded.

She opened the door a little farther, apparently convinced that I wasn't a salesman. I noticed she was wearing slippers, and I heard some loud daytime talk show on a television.

"I'm Ethan," I said, extending a hand. She didn't move to shake my hand and instead just looked at it.

"I'm Sue," she replied in steady tone, looking me up and down slowly.

It occurred to me that it is a little strange that after a few months, we hadn't met any of our neighbors; on the other hand, it did seem like a place where people keep to themselves.

"How you folks like living over in that house?" she asked.

"Oh, it's fine. We like it here in North Bend." I forced a smile. *Why were so many people so interested in how we liked living in the house?*

"Got any kids over there in that house?" Sue asked.

"No, no, we don't have any children." *What the hell did that have to do with anything?*

She nodded her head but didn't say anything. "Sometin' I can do for you?"

"Yes, actually...I need to get up into our attic, and we don't have a ladder. I was wondering if I could borrow yours, if you have one, that is."

Sue snorted in laughter and exhaled cigarette smoke through her nostrils. "Of course we have a ladder," she snapped.

She'd responded as if I offended her. I wasn't quite sure what to say, so a moment of silence passed between us. Rain started to fall, and my hair was already damp.

"Whatcha want to get up in yer attic for?" she asked.

"Oh, I just want to see what's up there. I think there are critters living in our house or something."

Sue snorted again and mumbled something under her breath that I couldn't quite make out, but it sounded as if she said something like "bet there are." *What did she mean to say by that remark?*

"Ladder's back on the side of the garage. You're welcome to it, but bring it back before the end of the day when my old man gets home. And put it back exactly where you find it. I'm not sure my husband would like me loaning out our ladder for free."

"Thank you, ma'am. I promise I'll just be a few minutes, and I'll bring it right back."

"And you be careful," she warned me. "Don't want you falling off our ladder and bringing over any bad luck to this house." Sue closed the door, leaving me standing in the then steady rainfall.

I found the ladder and walked back to our house. Sue's "loaning for free" comment was odd...Was this the kind of place where you charged your neighbors to borrow something? I had noticed when I went to grocery stores that people, in general, appeared to be thrifty, especially compared to spendy southern Californians. People in grocery store lines in western Washington appeared adamant to use their store membership cards, and many were armed with coupons, as well. I didn't recall ever seeing anyone even use a coupon while living in

California.

So they were a bit frugal and untrusting; no big deal. It was nice of her to let me borrow the ladder all the same. She could have dropped the house/kids interrogation, though. And what was more concerning was her comment on bringing back bad luck to her house. *Why on earth would she think that?*

I set it up outside the house, directly underneath the "secret window" at the front of the house. When I climbed up the ladder to where my face was even with the window, I saw that I was ill-equipped for the task. I remembered to grab a flashlight, but I thought that in order to open the window, I would just need to undo the small latch I'd noticed outside it. When I was up there, though, I stared at three nails that were pounded directly next to the window's opening and then purposefully bent inward in order to provide a tighter seal. It looked like whoever did it really wanted the window to remain closed and didn't plan on opening it again; they must have been worried about bats getting in there.

So I climbed down the ladder and ran through the driveway to the back of the house as quickly as I could. It did little good, though, as I was already fairly drenched. The rain was still falling in occasional torrents, and a chilly breeze was also contributing its efforts to the day's weather.

Although I had closed the door, it didn't lock unless locked from the inside. It led directly into the house's former "mud room," which was our laundry room. There were also some wooden cupboards in there that I used to store various things, such as my tool box. I grabbed a hammer and got back to the ladder.

I nearly lost my footing at one point while I was trying to pry back the nails, but I caught myself by grabbing the window's latch. When I looked down I noticed that if I had actually fallen, there was a very good possibility that I would have hit my head on the concrete stairs at the front door. That would have been bad. And I didn't even have health insurance because adding me on to Lib's insurance would have been really expensive.

With one last effort to bend back a nail, carefully so that that I didn't slip again, I was ready to open the secret window and finally look inside to see what awaited me in the dark.

I took a deep breath, turned on the flashlight, and opened the window.

Nothing…there was nothing in there. There were the wood beams of the house's ceiling and insulation stuffed between them, but there was nothing else from what I could see. I realized that bats could be hiding in any crevice, and I tried enticing them into revealing themselves by taking the hammer and banging on some of the interior wood to rattle them a bit, but there was no movement in response at all. I had expected to find a dank place complete with cobwebs, mold, and obvious signs of critter infestation. But it looked neat and orderly up there. I even noticed that the insulation in the ceiling appeared to be fairly new…so much for my theory that the house was so cold because of a lack of insulation.

There was nothing to see. As I was about to close the secret window, I suddenly lost my footing and slipped. I dropped the flashlight and braced my arms against the window frame.

Thankfully, the ladder didn't fall, and I was able to regain my footing. After steadying myself, I reached for the flashlight on top of the insulation inside, and I felt a sharp jab into my right arm followed by the unmistakable sensation of warm blood running down it. A trail of it flowed down my arm and spilled onto the white insulation surrounding the flashlight.

Carefully feeling around the inside of the window, I located what had cut me. I arched my head further into the window and used the flashlight to see that a rusty nail jutted out from below the window where I had braced myself. The damn thing had pierced me deeply, even through my coat, and the nail glimmered with my blood. *When was the last time I had a tetanus shot?*

I held my injured arm close against my side, hoping to stop the bleeding, and returned the ladder next door. I didn't see my newly acquainted neighbor, but the blinds fluttered a little as I walked by.

The wind picked up and bit at my face as I jogged back to the house. Even if it wasn't the warmest, I was looking forward to making a fire and sitting beside it with a book for a while.

Fuck. You've got to be kidding me! This was not possible. I tried the door again, only to confirm that it had somehow locked from the inside.

This was wonderful. I had no idea how it could have happened, but even the impossible was possible. Maybe I'd accidentally hit the lock with the hammer and somehow caused the lock to set. I had to admit that one way or another, I was really running into a lot of misfortune, and so much of it was aligned with the house.

One way or another, I was totally screwed. I didn't have my set of keys or cell phone with me. Fortunately, Lib had driven to work because she had a dentist appointment in the afternoon. I didn't have my watch on, but it must have been mid-afternoon, so it would not be too much longer before she returned home.

It was going to be cold and miserable sitting on the back steps waiting for her arrival, though, and I hoped the cut on my arm wasn't too bad. I wanted to look at it, but didn't want to take off my coat. I just held the general area firmly with my left hand.

I noticed Mrs. Pendergrass out in the yard watching me. She was crouched low to the ground in the long grass with her ears pinned back. I took a seat. "At least I have some company," I said to her.

* * * *

Why would Ethan be outside in this miserable weather? It had to be in the low forties, and why he'd ever want to be outside made absolutely zero sense. He was standing underneath the back patio area, but with the wind blowing, I doubted he was staying very dry. And with the lack of smoke coming out from the chimney, he'd obviously not even started a fire. *Great.* The house was going to be especially freezing. Seeing him out there and knowing that the fire wasn't started instantly put me in a bad mood.

"What the hell are you doing, Ethan?" I asked after I parked and opened the door, having to basically yell to be heard over the howling wind.

"I got locked out of the house earlier today," he called out in response.

I gathered my bags and quickly ran to the front door. "How?" He ran from the back to meet me.

"I have no idea," he said as he opened the screen door and moved aside so I could use my keys to unlock the door. "Somehow, the back door locked itself when I went to the neighbor's next door to borrow a ladder."

I opened the door and met with a blast of chilled air. At that point, I didn't even care to hear his excuses and was more concerned with him starting a fire immediately. "Well, let's get the fire going because it's freezing in here."

While he started piling wood and paper in the stove, Ethan told me his tale of how the back door that doesn't lock from the outside somehow miraculously locked itself and how he didn't see anything suspect in the attic. Both were hard to believe, and I'm sure he did something to lock the door, even if he didn't recognize his own fault. One thing he surely had not lied about, though, was cutting his arm. When he showed it to me, I was surprised he had gashed himself so deeply. I told him he needed to clean it immediately, and for a moment, I felt sorry for him.

That changed when I went back to the bedroom to change, finding the bedroom door closed again! I don't know how many times I'd told him to keep it open both for warmth and air circulation. *Why can't he just do what I ask?*

As I searched through my closet, looking for some warm, comfortable clothes to change into, I was greeted with another unpleasant surprise. There was mold on some of my clothes! I shrieked, and Ethan came into the bedroom and finding me tearing out clothes from my closet that had been infected. He checked his closet and found similar results, and then we both checked the closet in the in-between room, where we kept shoes, and discovered numerous pairs covered with mold, as well.

Utterly disgusted, I gave up and retreated to the couch to wrap myself in three blankets and asked Ethan to pour me a glass of wine, a large one. It was Friday, our pizza and movie night, but this wasn't even comforting to me. It had really not been a good day.

* * * *

The next day, we woke up early and got the SUV packed with our ski gear. Ethan made a nice breakfast for us, and after a good night's sleep, I didn't feel as irritated with him. I was glad to be getting out of the house for the day and actually felt better on the drive east on Highway 90 up to the ski resort. There were even some times when the clouds parted ways and allowed for moments of sunshine, and it was wonderful to see a little sun, however briefly.

The ski resort was smaller than we expected and was super crowded. The snow was heavier and wetter than the snow in California we'd encountered before, but considering how we were still really in the beginning category of skiing, we weren't disappointed. We spent a day watching each other fall and had more laughs together than we'd had in months. The sun continued to reveal its existence sporadically, and we didn't even mind waiting in the long lift lines.

After a long day on the slopes, we drove back down the pass. When we made it to North Bend, it was raining. Although neither of us said it, I had the feeling that we both wished we were still skiing. The house felt even colder than normal, and the strange odors I noticed at times in certain rooms were even more pronounced throughout the house.

I mentioned to Ethan that we didn't see the rabbit, whatever goofy name that Ethan had given it, as often in the yard. He mentioned that he had seen Mrs. Pendergrass on the day that he had been locked out of the house, but not since. Ethan thought that the presence of the cats around our house must have scared her off.

That reflection seemed to produce a spark in Ethan. After he put away our ski gear in the storage shed, he walked around the house, closely examining its exterior.

I personally didn't enjoy starting or maintaining the fire, but he was probably trying to solve our feline issues and was out there in the freezing rain, so I didn't mind trying to get the fire going. I started stoking paper and wood in the stove and tried to get a flame going…after numerous attempts, I then understood why Ethan always said that it was so difficult. Whenever I believed I had it started and I walked away for a minute, I returned only to find it never actually started.

I saw Ethan through the cold room's windows carrying some boards from the shed toward the back of the house. He came inside a few minutes later with a look of triumph on his face.

"You look like you've figured something out," I commented.

"Yup, think so," he responded as he peeled off his wet clothing in the laundry room. "There was an opening to underneath that little patio thing that's back there outside of our bedroom door window. I think the cats were getting in there at night. I covered up all potential access to it now, though, so I think that should take care of our late night cat parties."

I've never even walked around our yard, and I wasn't going to start in the rain. I took his word for it. "That's great, Ethan. I guess we'll find out if it works or not tonight."

"Yeah, guess we'll see. Hopefully, though."

"Well, good job. Now if you can figure out the rodent situation, too, we'll just have the cold, weird-smelling, mold issues left to face."

"One at a time, Lib. One at a time," Ethan responded with a smile. I wasn't sure if it was a forced smile or not.

****

There were, thankfully, no more nighttime cat visits after that. Ethan told me a couple of days later that he saw Mrs. Pendergrass outside again. He also went to a hardware store one day not long after our first ski day and bought a bunch of rodent poison, which he scattered all around the house. Someone at the hardware store told Ethan that while we most likely had mice, we probably also had a field rat infestation, due to the relatively rural location of our house. Ethan said that he found a bunch of holes in the yard, which indicated the presence of those even nastier things. He put the poison chunks in all of the holes and then filled them with rocks. It didn't seem to work completely, as I still heard the occasional scurrying, but we noticed a significant decrease. *Sure, it seemed unusual to have a cat and a rodent infestation, but what did I know?*

Even without the damn cats and rodents waking us up in the middle of the night, I still had trouble sleeping. I found myself waking up suddenly nearly every night at exactly the same time: 3:33 a.m. And whenever I did, I felt like my body was overheating.

Chapter 4

January

Christmas passed as just any other day, similar to Thanksgiving, but without a crazy snowstorm. We invited both of our sets of parents to visit us, but I think they were all mortified to come visit us during the rainy season, especially when we described how cold our house was even with a firing blazing away in the stove. *So much for being cooked out!*

    I was sure that any parental visits would be limited to the only month my coworkers told me was sure to have pleasant weather: August. Apparently even then though, there was still a chance for some icky days.

    I would have been so happy to at least have some decent days mixed in with our normal gray skies. I had never thought I would be the type to suffer from seasonal depression, but I was beginning to feel its cold fingers wrapping themselves around my neck. I think Ethan did too, but we didn't talk about it. I imagined he felt the same way, that discussing it wasn't going to do any good. We just kept barreling through and remained hopeful that the next month would be better, as we kept being told, yet waited to see for ourselves. Every month that passed so far had been the coldest month on record with most days of rain and lack of sun. *How could it just keep getting colder and darker?* I could understand that perhaps it was an off season of exceptionally foul conditions, but could it really be all that much better in normal years?

The initial honeymoon with my job had passed, and although I still enjoyed it most days, it was not nearly as exciting to me anymore. With the building stress from it, a couple days away from everything would do wonders, I thought. I didn't want to tell Ethan about how I was feeling about my job, though. I thought it would depress him to hear that I was already growing a little tired of my job when he hadn't even been able to find one. Since we had moved, I'd noticed that he was becoming a lot more sensitive.

A woman at my office told me about the town of Leavenworth, and we drove there to splurge a little and celebrate New Year's there together. A night away from the house and our routine would be good for us, and I managed to find a fairly good rate on a hotel room as we were staying on New Year's Day instead of the more sought after New Year's Eve.

Getting there was a little treacherous driving over a remote mountain pass after we turned off I-90, but we made it, and I was so glad that we had our new vehicle. When we first arrived, we checked into our hotel on the outskirts and then walked downtown together. We held hands the entire time, albeit wearing winter gloves, and it occurred to me that this was something we had not been doing as much.

The entire town was a replication of a Bavarian village, and even oil change places had signs with some sort of German-looking twist. The downtown area itself was extremely charming, complete with Bavarian-style building facades and horse drawn carriage rides in the streets. There were still Christmas decorations and lights hung everywhere. With the few inches of snow on the ground and it covering the surrounding mountainous peaks, the place definitely felt festive, and I liked it. I think Ethan did, as well; we didn't get this kind of experience in Southern California, after all.

We had a nice time strolling along the picturesque streets of the town, stopping in for a taste of chocolate here, a little wine tasting there, to pass through an art gallery, or to check out the wide array of interesting trinket shops. Ethan made a comment that if the Bavarian setting was replaced with coastal California, he would believe we were on Cannery Row in Monterey, where we also visited on our trip to San Francisco.

"Have you ever noticed how there are always stores selling fudge in touristy places like this?" Ethan observed.

"You know, I've never really thought about that until now, but now that you mention it, that's true."

"And they always advertise it so prominently in such places as this. It's almost like they just know that they are going to catch the interest of many people who would otherwise probably never eat fudge, but since they are on vacation in a touristy destination like this, they figure they will cut loose and indulge in some gooey, sugary substance that will stick to the tops of the mouths and get all over the sides of their face."

I laughed at his anti-fudge diatribe. "I didn't know you disliked it so much."

Ethan responded with a contorted look on his face. "Yuck. I don't know how anyone can even eat that stuff."

Just as he made this remark, a couple of overweight women stepped out of a doorway with gigantic wedges of fudge in their hands. They both took a bite of their respective fudge squares as they stepped onto the sidewalk and managed to get chocolate on the sides of their faces. We burst into laughter, the kind of uncontrolled laughter that is normally associated with children or drunken adults, and had to cross the street to a little park in order to escape the flurry of stares we received from people passing us on the sidewalk.

"How about lunch?" I proposed after our shared laugh gradually died down.

"Sure, that sounds great." Ethan checked his watch. "Well, it's just after three now, so it will be more like lunch and dinner combined."

"Linner!"

Ethan laughed again. "That's a good one, Lib."

We ended up randomly picking one of the numerous restaurants along the town's main strip that had their menus on display outside their doors offering "traditional Bavarian cuisine." Ethan ordered a plate with three different kinds of sausage, sauerkraut, and potato salad. I picked a stuffed cabbage dish. We both had a couple of large Hofbräu beers and took a few goofy photos of one another. By the end of our dinner, we both felt like stout Germans and were slightly tipsy from the strong beer.

It had turned to night by the time we left the restaurant, and there was a chill in the air; light snowflakes were falling. Amidst the town's Christmas lights strung over the streets and outside of the building facades, the snow created a lovely scene. We stopped into a couple of bars and sampled a few more different German beers. Later, we slowly made our way back to our hotel room.

We started watching a movie on the hotel's television while sitting in bed, but we barely saw more than a few minutes of it. Instead, we made passionate love and both fell soundly asleep not long after.

It had been a wonderful weekend escape, and I didn't want to return to the house in North Cloud.

*****

Whenever we caught a slight break and things began to look better, something happened to turn everything in the wrong direction once again. Somehow, our house tended to be involved.

Our short trip to Leavenworth had been great; we actually had fun together again. As we pulled into our driveway, I felt tension building between us for no real reason. It was as if the house had a bad mood of its own that captured us in its gloomy shadow.

Stepping into the house just made things worse. It felt like a damned ice cave. I chose to get a fire going before unpacking, a strategy Libby didn't appear to mind. Later, as I was taking the suitcase out to the storage shed, I discovered that its side window had been broken. The door was closed, but unlocked. Whoever broke in there must have climbed in through the window and then left out the door. *How nice of them to have closed it.*

I quickly surveyed the interior of the shed before I went inside to tell Libby of the break-in. It looked like they'd stolen our skis, boots, helmets, bikes, golf clubs, and even our snorkeling gear. Aside from the patio furniture that we kept out there, they'd pretty much cleaned the place out.

Libby was infuriated when I showed her. Although I couldn't blame her, I didn't see the point in getting upset. There was nothing we could do about it. The worst part was that with all of our ski stuff gone, it was going to be a while before we could get back on the slopes. Instead of skiing excursions, we could now look forward to notifying our rental insurance company and dealing with all of that sure-to-be fun. *Awesome.*

I covered up the broken window with cardboard and told Libby that I'd call the sheriff's office first thing in the morning to report the break-in. I remembered how helpful he'd been last time. I couldn't wait.

*****

Why was it that I had the impression that this sheriff just didn't like me for some reason? I'd never been one to have a problem with law enforcement types, and I'd always viewed them as helpful and understanding; this officer presented neither quality.

"I see you got Washington tags for your vehicle finally," were the first words he said to me as I stepped out the front door to meet him.

"And this is a new vehicle, as well," he said as walked around our small SUV. "Yup, looks pretty nice." The way he said it bothered me for some reason. Like he resented us for it.

"Thank you, and thank you for coming out this morning," I remarked.

"You bet...What seems to be the problem this time?"

Did the dispatcher not inform you that this visit of yours is regarding a home burglary? Is this not supposed to be part of your job functions in protecting and serving the local citizens?

"This time, someone broke into our storage shed over there," I said, pointing in the direction of the shed at the end of the driveway.

"Oh really? Well, let's take a look, then."

I led him to the shed. "We were gone for a couple of days over the weekend, and when we returned, I found this side window here busted out and the door unlocked. When I went inside, I saw that whoever did this had pretty well cleaned us out. We had a lot of our recreational gear in here: skiing things, bikes, golf clubs, and some other stuff."

"What kind of other stuff?" he quickly asked.

"Snorkeling equipment," I answered plainly.

"Ah, well, it wasn't really cleaned out entirely, now was it? There are still a couple of boxes over there and a few luggage items it looks like that are still here."

Two things bothered me about his comments. One, I noticed that he was not referring to anyone having actually conducted the robbery when he said "it wasn't" instead of "they didn't." Second, the sheriff was focusing on what was remaining, rather than what had been stolen. "I actually just put that suitcase in here after our weekend trip," I coldly pointed out.

The sheriff looked at me with a straight face, and it was difficult to sense what he was thinking. "Okay, well, we'll file a police report that you can use for insurance purposes. Was the main house broken into at all, or did you notice any signs of attempted entry into it?"

"No."

"Did you keep that flood light on by your back door while you were away?"

"No, we didn't. We kept on the light above the front door," I responded.

The sheriff shook his head, and I thought I noticed him roll his eyes. "I'd leave it on from now on when you're gone," he stated more than recommended. "Have you ever noticed anyone suspicious around your house in the last few weeks?"

"Not exactly...but in the house just down from us, there's suspicious activity occurring that I notice from time to time." As I spoke, I walked back to the driveway and pointed in the direction of the house I'd mentally labeled a possible meth house.

"Have you ever reported this?" he asked from behind me.

"Well, no. We're just trying to be good neighbors and mind our own business."

"True enough. People round these parts do mind their own business, and they don't make accusations that they can't back up."

I was being lectured after I had just answered his question?

"You mean that house right over there?" he asked.

"Yeah, that little blue house with the unmaintained yard and all of the garbage around it."

"Frank Sounder's boy, Sam, lives there with his girlfriend. Frank's an old friend of mine, and his boy has never been in any trouble. Why would you think Sam would possibly have anything to do with this?"

Because meth heads seem to have a propensity to take up stealing for drug money, last I heard.

"Well, I'm just saying that the house is suspicious to me: they let their dogs run wild outside; there's often music blaring from over there in the middle of the day; I've never seen any blinds open; and there are different cars coming and going all day over at times." I instantly regretted having shared my opinion and realized I was about to be slammed in response.

"Son, you're making some pretty mighty accusations there. We're not inner city Seattle out here, and if you haven't noticed, a lot of people let their dogs run around their yards. As long as that so-called loud music isn't happening at night, they aren't breaking any noise ordinances. Whether or not they open their blinds implies nothing. A lot of us keep our blinds closed in winter to keep as much heat in our homes as possible. I know Sam got laid off from his job recently, and if he has friends coming over to his house some days to see him, there's no crime in having friends, either. So, like you said, you'd better stick to your own business and leave police work to me." He walked to his police cruiser and opened the driver side door. "I'll write up my report later on today, and you can call over to the office to request a copy of it. You have yourself a good day now."

He didn't give me a chance to reply before hopping into his car.

The sheriff turned out of our driveway onto the street. I looked up and noticed that the rocky peak of Mount Si was partially visible between layers of clouds for a few moments before it was once again engulfed and disappeared. It started to rain again.

* * * *

Our weekend away in Leavenworth was wonderful, and I wished the happiness we felt together could have lasted longer. Instead, within days after our return, the grinding tension between Ethan and me inexplicably returned. Whenever I got home from work, I instantly felt annoyed with him, and I didn't know really why. It was frustrating that he was still barely working from home.

He did start a fire before he picked me up at the bus stop, and he prepared dinner so that it'd be ready soon after we returned. He even did some house cleaning, which he never used to do. So, all in all, I realized that I shouldn't be so hard on him because he was doing what he could, but still…still, there was something about him that just irritated me more often than not. I couldn't help it, even if I tried ignoring it.

Then, one day, I was standing in the rain at the bus stop waiting for him to get off his ass and come and get me. He was normally there when I stepped off the bus. The umbrella wasn't keeping all the rain off me because the wind was blowing so hard. It was freezing. *Where was he? How could he be stupid enough to forget to pick me up, the same as he has nearly every weekday for a couple of months?*

Just as I was about to get my cell phone out of my purse to call him, I saw him turn at the intersection and drive toward the parking area where I was waiting. "Where the fuck were you?" I demanded to know as soon as I stepped into the vehicle.

"Whoa, sweetie, I'm sorry. I tried to get my weekly grocery shopping in before picking you up and got stuck in a long line at the store with some old grandma demanding everything be separately bagged and then taking an hour to find all of her coupons and write a check. And then I got caught behind some super slow cars getting back over here."

Pathetic excuses, I said to myself. "Ethan, you have all day to go to the store. Why would you even begin to think that it was a good idea to wait until the end of the day to go, especially when you know that if you don't come get me, I'm going to be stranded in the rain?"

"Lib, it wasn't raining earlier, but you're right, and I apologize. It was a bad idea."

"So why didn't you call me and let me know?"

"I left my cell phone in the car while I was in the store."

"You could have called me as soon as you left the store."

"Yes, you're right, I could have, but I was just trying to get over here as fast as I could."

I was still fuming mad when we got home. *I was the one working all day, and he couldn't even be on time to pick me up? This was unacceptable.*

"So how many jobs did you apply to today?" I inquired as I set my bags down near the door.

Ethan shrugged his shoulders. "None. I mean, I didn't find any to apply to."

"Did you even look?" I quickly snapped back.

"I look every day, Lib," he weakly responded.

I assumed he was lying. "Just find a job!" I yelled at him.

"I'm trying!" he yelled.

"Well, you need to try harder!" I'd had enough, so I went straight to the refrigerator. I pulled out a bottle of wine and poured myself a glass. I was going to take a long bath and get away from him for a while. I didn't even care about what happened in there last time. I wanted some time by myself.

As I passed the wood burning stove on my way toward the back of the house, I noticed Ethan's shoe footprints on the hardwood floor once again. I was about to scream at him about it, but passing by the stove, I also noticed something strange…there was what appeared to be an outline of a large hand on the top of the stove, like when someone places their hand on glass for a while and then removes it. The black cast iron stove must have been searing hot, so Ethan certainly hadn't put his hand there recently. He must have earlier, and somehow, it was just showing up in the half light.

It was still weird though…and if I hadn't been so pissed off with Ethan, I would have said something to him about it. I grew even more upset when I looked toward the bedroom and saw that he had once again closed its door. I didn't want to say another word to him that evening.

* * * *

We were off to a great start to the week. Lib didn't say a word to me after our argument last night, and she still was peeved this morning when I dropped her off at the bus stop. I was tempted to say something, but thought it better not to. Libby didn't get riled up too often about things, but I'd learned that it was better for me to step back when she did. No matter what I said, it would never do any good.

She even took a bath for the first time since she had months ago, which meant she must have been really pissed off at me, because she wouldn't have gone back in there otherwise. I knew she was apprehensive to take another bath after the first time. Thankfully, there was no drama involved with her bathtub experience this time, but I was definitely on edge as I heard her start the water. I couldn't relax the entire time she was in there.

It was snowing lightly, and I watched Mrs. Pendergrass run across the yard from my window. I had some blog research work to keep me busy for a few hours, but not enough for a full day. I planned go for a walk later down the road as I did pretty much every day around noon.

Besides, I deserved a nice walk. I had secured a new cord of wood for us to burn. Libby had been insistent that I demand that we only receive dry wood and that it be delivered at a time when it was not raining so that it didn't get wet. Considering that it was pretty much raining all the time or was about to, I figured her second demand was probably not going to be met, but I stressed the first.

It was hard to believe we'd already burned through one cord of wood, but I had no doubt that we'd burn through another. And I hadn't yet told Libby that I had found a good price for the new cord and even got the guy to deliver it for free…so maybe she wouldn't think I was such a loser when I told her after she got home from work.

I hoped that would be the case, and I wanted to fully enjoy my walk. On my walk, I had grown used to the various dogs that came out barking like crazy at me. Often, I got soaked when I went. Even if it was snowing, it would be wet snow that drenched my clothing, but I didn't mind, and I used the opportunity to gather small sticks alongside the road that I used to start the fire. I always felt good getting out of the house for the forty minutes or so it took me to walk down to the end of the road to the highway overpass and back. I liked seeing the horses in the fields down there and saw an elk, usually a small of group of them, on a routine basis.

At first, I got really excited seeing them, but I think I grew accustomed to it. I still, however, marveled at their size. If people weren't used to being close to elk, I doubted they realized their size. They were roughly twice the size, at least, of any typical deer. At first, I emailed photos to Libby of the elk I would see, but then I stopped doing it. I think she was annoyed with me when I did, like she believed I should be spending every free moment I had on the job search. Also, I think she was a little jealous of me being able to take walks during the middle of the day. But if I had been her, I would have taken advantage of lunch breaks to walk around downtown.

She still loved seeing elk, though. One morning, as I was making coffee for her to take on the bus, there was a herd of over twenty elk in the field behind our house. I quickly got her to follow me from her bathroom, where she was getting ready. She was very impressed…and it was impressive. We had twenty of those enormous animals strut by our front door in single file. It was one of those sights that one never forgets.

Sometimes, although rarely, the clouds would partially clear, and I'd be able to see Mt. Si and Mt. Tenerife next to it, as I had learned it was called, towering over me on one side and Rattlesnake Ridge stretching across the horizon on the other. The perpetual gray and gloomy clouds that provided a backdrop to most scenes pretty much disintegrated all scenic qualities of the place.

As I gazed outside in reflection, a couple of deer entered the yard. After having grown so used to seeing elk so close, I wasn't all that impressed with the mere sight of a deer. But they were just outside my room's window within touching distance, and that was unique. They were right there, less than a few feet away, and they didn't realize I was right next to them.

What the hell? I hadn't moved at all or done anything to call attention to myself, but all of a sudden, both deer quickly looked up directly at me, and they were instantly spooked. Just the sight of me sitting in my room for some reason caused them such fright that they instantly darted away from the house toward the street. They were so scared that they clumsily ran into one another, and one them rammed into the wooden fence surrounding our yard. Seconds later, I heard the unmistakable sound of a car slamming on its brakes just beyond the front bushes, followed immediately by the equally unmistakable and awful thud of a vehicle hitting something made of flesh and bone.

I hurriedly grabbed a coat, pulled on my boots, and rushed out the front door to the street. A huge patch of the formerly white show layering the road has been turned to crimson red in front of a pickup truck on the side of the road where it had slid to a stop. The driver of the vehicle, a middle-aged woman, appeared to be in a state of shock. She just sat in her truck. I knocked on her side window, and she rolled it down slowly.

I asked if she was okay, to which she replied that she was fine. She said that she would call the sheriff's office on her cell phone to report the accident. A strange noise then caught my attention.

Moving to the front of the truck, I saw where the noise was emanating from. One of the deer was writhing in agony near the side of the road, covered in its own blood spewing from its chest. As the animal struggled on the ground, a low guttural sound escaped from its mouth. When its eyes saw me, the deer appeared to spasm even more intensely. Within a few moments, it stopped moving altogether, and its head fell slightly backward to the ground.

I offered to stay with the woman in the truck until the sheriff arrived. When he did, he merely shook his head in my direction, as if I somehow had caused the deer to run out in front of the truck. As I could clearly see that I was no longer of use, and since after standing outside for twenty minutes, I was freezing my butt off, I announced that I was heading inside. Neither of them acknowledged my parting.

I decided to walk through the yard back to our house, through the small opening between our front bushes and the side fence where the deer had sprung out from earlier. I then realized that this was actually the first time I'd walked into the yard this way. As I rounded the corner of the hedges, I saw my room, and there was my window with the computer desk on the other side of it. *But what the hell was that?* It looked like there was an old man standing in my room directly behind the computer desk!

Feeling momentarily petrified with fear, I just stood there staring into my room. I didn't see what I saw anymore, but I was still feeling scared shitless. Summoning some courage, I took a deep breath and started walking slowly toward the window. When I made it there, I took another deep breath and peered inside. Nothing looked out of the ordinary...but then I remembered that when I first ran out of the house, I had left the front door open wide. After assessing the situation on the road, I went back to grab my set of keys and closed the front door. *Could someone have gotten into the house during those few minutes?*

I felt fear return, coupled with mounting panic as I walked around the side of the house. Looking inside the living room window, I didn't see anything. It had been snowing the entire time, so if someone had indeed snuck inside the house, there would be noticeable footprints leading to our front door. Maybe someone could have followed my own footprints, but there would still be footprints leading from down the street. And if someone did slip inside, the sheriff was just around the corner. Even if he didn't like me for some reason, he'd have to come over if I said I believed there was an intruder inside our house.

But when I reached our driveway's entrance from the street, there were no footprints coming from either direction that could not have been my own. The sheriff, still standing outside the lady's truck, was talking to her and taking notes; he glanced over at me but quickly turned away again.

When I stepped back inside our house, I still didn't feel totally at ease, and the hair on the back of my neck was raised. I closed the front door quietly and started craning my neck to look into the other rooms. I tiptoed to the kitchen and pulled out our one and only large carving knife. I then proceeded to check every room, inside every closet, even under our bed and inside the shower, knife in hand. When I was lifting the comforter hanging down the side of the bed, I realized how ridiculous I was being...*was I looking for the boogeyman?*

Libby would definitely be interested to hear the deer crash story, but I thought I'd leave out me creeping through the house with a butcher knife, scared out of my wits. With the way things had been going between us most of the time, she'd probably just laugh at me if I told her that story, and not in a nice way.

* * * *

That was an earthquake, no doubt about it. We'd experienced enough during our time in California to recognize one, and what had just happened was no different. It woke both of us up, and the shake caused Libby to cross the bed and lay her head on my shoulder and put her arms around my neck. I wouldn't say she had a real phobia of earthquakes, but she got pretty freaked out by them. I grabbed my cell phone, which also served as my alarm clock, and saw that it was 3:33 a.m. *Hadn't Libby told me something about her waking up some nights around this time?* And I couldn't figure out at all why I was sweating...It was cold in the bedroom. *And what was the odd smell I noticed?*

The earthquake was like many we'd encountered before, with a sudden jolt that temporarily rattles everything within a household, including one's equilibrium. This one felt different for us, though, in that we had always been in relatively modern apartment buildings compared to our old little farm house here in North Bend. Those buildings felt secure in quakes, for the most part. The house, on the other hand, took an exceptionally long time to adjust to the bolt of movement that had accelerated through the ground beneath it, and it settled in a series of creaks and groans, almost as if it were coming alive.

I tried to fall asleep again, yet found my mind persisted to swirl with dark thoughts...*Didn't the Green River Killer, America's own Jack the Ripper, commit his evil deeds in Western Washington?* I thought Ted Bundy started off his killing spree in the Seattle area, as well. *Was it odd that two of the country's most notorious and ferocious serial killers originated from the same place?* I even recalled that one of Canada's most gruesome serial killers operated in the Vancouver area—an area not far and one that shared Western Washington's climate. *It had to be the weather.*

The image of the little piece of strange pottery with what looked like a spot of blood on it I had found in the house popped into my head, and I felt a strange chill move through me. I closed my eyes but couldn't get that damn image to go away. I shivered at the thought of it.

In the morning, after a near sleepless night, I dropped Libby off at the bus stop in a downpour of icy rain. When I was back at the house, I checked the U.S. Geological Survey to find out details on the earthquake that previous night. It was odd...but there were no listings for an earthquake having occurred anywhere near us in weeks. It must have been too soon. Perhaps it was such a small one that they weren't rushed to post the details. I spent a few hours doing some research for an editor from my company and then did yet another fruitless job search. I later checked again for some info on the quake Still there was nothing.

Chapter 5

February

I'd heard people I work with say that often in the month of February, the region experienced a temporary reprieve of sorts from the perpetual onslaught of rain and gloom. Considering that so far, we had just kept hearing how each month set some new record for foul weather, such a prediction was more than welcome. After the previous few months, I was not sure I really believed it, but so far, February had indeed presented a few strings of days where it was actually sunny and almost pleasant. On those days, the temperature still hovered in the fifties, but a day in the fifties with sunshine in the middle of February after what we'd encountered was a blessing.

I'd gotten into the habit of taking a long hot bath with a glass of wine after work a few nights a week. Aside from its normal coldness, we'd experienced few new issues with the house. The new cord of wood that Ethan got for us was drier than the last. At least Ethan was able to get a fire lit more quickly than before and keep it going. His poor hands and wrists were already covered in scars from where he'd burned himself tending the fire.

Ethan had a few interviews for positions early in the month, and he felt very positive about his prospects. And as far as our relationship was concerned, we even took a turn for the better and hadn't argued once in weeks. This was also extremely welcome, since I was honestly getting to the point where I doubted our compatibility for the first time. Such thoughts troubled me. I wanted nothing more than to spend my life with him.

* * * *

It was the last weekend of the month, and I decided that we could use another jaunt away. Ethan believed he would find out about the two jobs he interviewed for the next week, and I was feeling hopeful for us. We couldn't really afford an expensive long weekend trip, but I found a cheap online price for a hotel outside of Vancouver, British Columbia, and suggested to Ethan that we just go for it and worry about our gradually mounting credit card debt later.

I guess I didn't really know what to expect from Vancouver. It had the reputation of being a gorgeous city and for being an increasingly popular destination for the shooting of Hollywood movies; Ethan told me this about it. Even though the city was located relatively close to the U.S. border, I assumed that, being in a different country after all, it would have a completely different feel than Seattle. After all, when we used to head down to Baja on weekends from San Diego, there was no doubt we were in a different country. Truthfully, though, it didn't feel much different than being in the States.

I took off Friday afternoon so we could drive up and arrive at our hotel that night and be able to get an early start seeing the city the next morning. A lot of people I worked with raved about going skiing at Whistler outside of the city, but there was no way we could afford the pricey lift passes on top of what we were already spending for the weekend trip. The drive north was fairly uneventful, but we were somewhat surprised at the amount of traffic we encountered, and we spent quite a bit of time waiting at the border crossing.

We spent the day trying to experience as much as we could. We started off with a walk and picnic in beautiful Stanley Park. The sky was blue and sun was shining, and it felt like a spring day. We sat near the water and watched the seaplanes come and go from the city's harbor. Next, we went to check out the Convention Center. Ethan read it was highly recommended, but once we were there, we weren't quite sure what was so special about the place, aside from the sweeping views of the harbor and the towering snow-capped mountains directly east of the city.

In the fleeting moments when the sky momentarily cleared from my office in downtown Seattle, I had seen the Olympics, the Cascades, Puget Sound, and Mount Rainier surrounding me…I didn't honestly know if I had ever encountered a more scenic place. Unfortunately, this had only happened a couple of times; when it had, the view vanished within minutes. However, I had to admit that Vancouver did offer its own majestic beauty, and the closer proximity of the mountains to the east was impressive, as the high ridges appeared to loom directly over the waters of the harbor.

The Gastown district was our next stop, and we found it to be a charming little area with cute shops, restored buildings, and brick sidewalks.

"This kind of reminds of the Pioneer Square area in Seattle," I mentioned to Ethan as we snacked on salmon hot dogs from an Asian street vendor. It sounded too interesting to not try.

"From what I've read, it's a lot safer up here," Ethan answered. "What do you think of the salmon hot dog?"

I took another bite and thought about it for a moment before answering. I replied, "Hmm, well, it tastes like a hot dog made with ground up salmon."

Ethan laughed. "Yeah, pretty much what you'd expect. Should we head over to Chinatown?"

"Well, from what the visitor information guy over at the Convention Center told us, it's kind of a walk, and he advised not being down there after dark, which, even though it's still sunny now, probably isn't far off; it is still February after all, and we're even more north than normal."

"Good point. How about a stroll down that Robson Street that he suggested?"

"Sure," I agreed.

After consulting our little tourist map, we began walking in the direction of Robson Street. "Things have been better so far this month, don't you think?" I asked Ethan as we walked, holding hands.

"They have. I'm started to feel better about everything."

I grinned and rested my head briefly on his shoulder.

As the afternoon grew chilly. we decided we had had enough sightseeing for the day, drove through the excruciating line of traffic to cross the Lions Gate Bridge, and returned to our hotel located in a non-descript area of car dealerships, roadside restaurants, and hotels. After cleaning up a bit, we decided to drive around until we found an interesting, and hopefully cheap, restaurant for dinner.

We decided on a small Vietnamese restaurant with a huge fish aquarium in its center and enjoyed an array of delicious food. Ethan commented that someday, we should take a trip to Vietnam, and I thought it sounded like a wonderful idea.

The next morning, we were up early, and we drove to the famed Capilano Suspension Bridge. It was cool to walk across the hanging bridge hundreds of feet above the river below and being surrounded by towering pine trees. We walked around the forest and did the "tree walk," but seriously, for as much as they charged for entry into the place, it was definitely a once in a lifetime event.

Considering that the drive up took longer than we had expected, after our visit to Capilano, we started back to Washington. It had been a good little visit to Seattle's neighbor in the north, but I wanted to get home in time to have a little relaxation time before heading back to work the next morning.

* * * *

It seemed kind of amazing how, the closer we got to North Bend, the cloudier it became. Our quick trip to Vancouver had been fun, and I wished we could have stayed longer. When we pulled into our driveway, there was a steady downpour of rain, and I knew that Lib was dreading how cold the house would be as much as I was. And the damned front light over the door that we had left on had gone out again. As we stepped into the house, I felt all of the good emotions we'd shared in the last couple of days begin to disintegrate.

But all in all, things were looking up for us, and the great trip we'd just had indicated to that the next month was going to be a good one for us. We kept hearing from people that March was nowhere near as bad of weather as earlier in the season. I just knew one of the positions I interviewed for was going to work out.

After I brought in our backpacks and suitcase from the car, I got a fire started with relative ease, and Libby said she was going to take a bath. I heard her say something about me having left the bedroom door closed as she walked toward the back of the house, but I knew that I purposefully left it open. I didn't even respond. There was a heater unit in her bathroom, so at least she'd stay warm in there as the house gradually warmed up a bit. Hopefully, that would make her happier.

I was eager to check my email to see if I'd received any responses from either company Friday afternoon. Opening the door to my room, I was instantly struck by an intuition: something was not right. I turned on the overhead light, which instantly burned out. The curtains were drawn, and I couldn't really see anything. I moved to switch on my small desk lamp, and as I did, something crunched beneath my feet.

Once the light was on, I saw that the crunching was from the glass picture frame I kept on my desk that had a picture of Libby and me on the day I proposed to her on a beach in La Jolla. *What the hell?*

Even if there had been an earthquake, there was no possible way it could have ended up there, as it was on the ground on the opposite end of the desk. Besides, if there had been an earthquake large enough to knock down this picture frame, there would undoubtedly be more things on the floor. Instead, there was just our picture on the ground, and it was on the wrong side of the desk. Now that I'd stepped on it, it was impossible to tell if the glass in the frame was already broken beforehand or not. A chill moved through me as I noticed that glass shards had punctured each of us in the photograph.

Setting the broken picture frame on the desk, I examined all of the windows and doors of the house to see if I could find any evidence of a break-in. Then I looked for anything else damaged or missing.

After thoroughly investigating, I found nothing else out of the ordinary and had to assume that somehow when I'd turned off my computer a couple of before, I must have accidentally swung my arm and knocked the picture frame down. It seemed improbable that I wouldn't have noticed doing it, but I supposed it was possible.

Although the picture frame quickly took a far second on my list of troubling discoveries of that day...

While I walked around the exterior of the house, looking for any indication of a forced a door or window open, I actually found something. There, on our back patio, was Mrs. Pendergrass's beheaded body.

After Libby got out of the bathtub, I told her the grave news. I'd already dug a hole in the backyard and buried the body, getting sufficiently drenched as I did. Libby asked how it could be possible that we had a dead rabbit on our back patio. I had purposefully left out the fact that Mrs. Pendergrass's head was nowhere to be found but responded that a hawk must have initially killed our bunny and dropped it while trying to carry it away. The hawk then was probably too skittish to come closer to the house to retrieve its prey. Lib appeared to be pacified by my explanation.

Finally able to check my email later, I was confronted with the disappointing news that I was no longer considered a candidate for either of the two positions. *Awesome...I couldn't wait for March.*

Chapter 6

March

I really missed the sun. Aside from a few scattered days, mostly in February, it had been either raining or gloomy with clouds from the moment we arrived. And even on the semi-decent days, which only counted if one considered a day to be semi-decent if it was partially sunny for a few hours, there had typically been other weather factors present, such as high winds or snow, in the equation. I'd felt cold since the day we moved to North Bend.

Everyone I worked with kept saying that the rainy season definitely would end in March. I was growing tired of constantly being told that "it's going to be nicer next month."

We were midway through March, and it was still rainy, gloomy, and chilly. And there was not even the benefit of it being lighter in the mornings or evenings, as with the near constant cloud cover, the days getting longer was unrecognizable.

I actually looked forward to leaving for work in the mornings and felt a sense of dread when I rode the bus home at the end of the day. Part of this, I blamed on the weather. Although it was only thirty miles away, North Bend was a different world than Seattle. This was true of the mentality, pace, character, and geography of the place. But it was also a fact I experienced daily that the weather patterns were also different. Seattle was never all that nice, but it was consistently a little less cloudy, less rainy, less dark, and less chilly. I wondered at times how we ended up in North Bend. I had begun noticing all of these pieces since the time we arrived, but by March, they were unmistakable.

Another thing I hated about going home was that even when Ethan had a fire going by the time I arrived, the house remained cold. I only felt warm when I crawled into bed and was under our heated blanket. Even then, I was already dreading waking up the next morning and having to get ready for work in the frigid air. Some mornings, it was so cold, I could even see my own breath!

And I felt like Ethan and I were drifting apart. We had fun on our weekend trips and when we went skiing together. But the day-to-day relationship had gotten worse and worse. And even though Ethan still often made dinner, most nights, he ate by himself before I came home, and then I ate alone.

After I ate, he rarely even wanted to sit down next to me on the couch to watch movies. Instead, he spent all of his time in that stinky office, playing on his computer, reading, or doing whatever he did in there. He spent all day in there. *Why did he want to spend evenings in there, too?* To me, it was becoming obvious that he was trying to entirely avoid me. I had heard this happened with older couples at times, but we'd only been married for a couple of years.

And obviously he was not spending much time looking for jobs, since he hadn't gotten any more interviews since February. Honestly, I was starting to think that he was purposefully sabotaging his job search. I opened the door to the office the other night, and I swear Ethan was just sitting, staring at the closed curtains. *Who did that?* When I asked him what he was doing, it took him a moment to respond, as if he had to consider his answer first. Then he defensively snapped back by asking if I couldn't see that he was "thinking." And it seriously smelled even worse in there than it did before. *I don't know how he can stand it.*

The mice scurrying around in our bedroom walls had gotten worse again, and they often woke me up. It was so unpleasant lying in bed with little feet scratching all around you. There was also a windmill next to a barn on a neighboring property that had started shrieking as the wind blew it. The noise was excruciating, like rusted metal grinding against itself. It reminded me of sounds associated with hell in horror films. Somehow, Ethan was able to sleep through it all, and that just further annoyed me.

Our weekends at home had gradually gotten worse, as well. The ski resort closed earlier than normal the second weekend of March, due to a lack of snowfall. It was hard to believe, but even though every day was cold with some amount of rain, it was apparently not cold enough in the mountains to turn to snow, so the ski slopes turned to slush. That eliminated a go-to outlet for us to get out of the house to do something we both enjoyed together.

On top of that, I couldn't even take my long baths during the week any longer. I could have, but I didn't want to anymore. One night, I was in my bathroom taking a bath when I felt something weird again. Nothing had occurred like before, but I had the undeniable feeling that I was being watched. I couldn't tell from where. But it creeped me out, and I didn't see myself taking a bath again for a while.

I reflected on all of this as I gazed out of my office window at rain drops streaking down the side of window. I looked at my watch and noticed it was time to catch my bus home from work. I wasn't looking forward to it at all. And I was sure the murder of crows that was now always surrounding our house would be there to greet me. I couldn't always see them on darker days when I got home later in the day, which I did purposefully at times, but I knew they were there.

****

I swore I kept hearing something coming from somewhere in the house, even when I had my headphones on. It was like a loud banging coming from somewhere near the bedroom. But every time I put my headphones down and walked over to check it out, there was nothing...except for the fact that the bedroom door always closed by itself, even if I propped it wide open, which I tried.

At first, I took one of Lib's shoes and put it next to the door, only to come back a couple of hours later and find the door closed, the shoe moved aside. I then tried out other objects, increasing the weight gradually, only to have the same result. When I put something really big in front of the door, like a chair, the door stayed open. So I went back to the shoe and sat there one day, for hours, just watching and waiting. Nothing happened. I left and came back later. The door was closed. It made me fear that someone was in the bedroom that really wanted the door closed, like they were locking themselves in there.

But that was bullshit. Clearly, it was just some sort of strange draft moving through the house that was strong enough to move a shoe, but not a chair. As with other things around the house, it began to amuse me when I saw it. When you spend all day every day all by yourself in an old house in the middle nowhere without much to do staring out at cloudy days...one can become easily amused. *Maybe I was spending too much time alone?*

I found myself more and more drawn to my room. I didn't even go on walks anymore; I didn't feel the motivation or enthusiasm. And it was not even the crappy weather keeping me inside. The weather was nothing different. It'd been continually crappy for months. I sat at my computer desk and waited for the days to pass.

One day, I thought something was tapping on the walls of my room. Turning my head from the computer screen, I watched a bird slam into the window outside. It was like watching the whole thing in slow motion. The glass didn't break, but the bird's outline clearly remained imprinted on the window. But when I walked over to the side of the room, expecting to see the bird downed in the wet grass outside, there was nothing.

I had an equally strange encounter with a raccoon another day. This huge raccoon strolled by just outside my room's window in our front yard. Maybe I would have expected that in the early morning or evening, since it was fairly dark still during both, but this happened during the middle of the day. I'd never seen a raccoon walking around in the daytime, so it was totally bizarre. After being initially shocked by the sight, I knocked on the window, and the raccoon merely looked at me curiously and then slowly climbed to a nearby tree on the other side of the yard. The raccoon found a perch on a branch where it just sat. Watching me.

After an hour of receiving a stare down from those dark eyes, I'd had enough and decide to scare the damn thing off somehow. As I passed through the living room, I accidentally ran into one of the large potted house plants, and a few of its dead leaves fell to the floor. This particular plant had replaced a previous one I had in the same spot that died earlier, which had actually equally replaced an earlier plant. Everything around me seemed to be dying.

Just as I was about to open the back door of the house, I remembered to grab my set of keys, just in case I somehow "locked myself out again," as Libby loved to so nicely put it whenever she was irritated with me. I stepped out to our back patio area through the rear door and noticed that there was one spot on Rattlesnake Ridge that was illuminated by the sun—just one distinct area of the entire evergreen forested ridge. The top of the ridge was entirely obscured by a low, gray cloud cover, but a single spot remained brightly illuminated with sunshine.

Water dripped from the overhang all around me. I had to be careful to avoid stepping on the huge slugs that had invaded everywhere surrounding our house. They had started to appear mid-way through the month, and they were disgusting things, with their shiny, thick trails of slime. When I made it around to the side of the house and looked upward in the tree where the raccoon had been, it was nowhere to be seen. *Was I seriously starting to imagine things?*

It was odd how I was comforted when I returned to my room and saw that the outline of the bird that had flown into the window was still there. At least I hadn't imagined that one. I felt a little bad for the bird and wondered what had happened to it, but it must have been okay and flown off. *But seriously, what the hell was it with the house and its influence on critters?* Anyway, just another death around this strange-ass house from hell, I figured.

* * * *

Libby was in the bedroom. I hadn't seen her go in there, but I knew it for some reason. I was in my room. I felt so languid and out of it; it was like I was watching myself from above. I rose from my desk, walked calmly to the kitchen, and took a kitchen knife from a drawer.

I walked through the in-between room to the bedroom. The door was closed. I looked down and noticed I was wearing big winter boots that I had never seen before.

Knife in hand, I slowly turned the knob on the bedroom door and stepped inside. I recognized my intentions. I would kill Libby.

I woke from the horrible daydream, my face and neck covered in sweat. I didn't remember doing it, but I must have put my head down on the desk to take a nap.

My left arm apparently had provided a pillow, and it had the dead sensation of being drained of blood. While I was asleep, my hand had knocked down the picture of Libby and me on my desk.

I didn't experience nightmares often, much less daydream nightmares, and I was unaccustomed to how real they could feel. I knew I could never do harm to Libby. *Why did my subconscious have me about to murder her? Were things between us really getting that bad? Or was it something else…something to do with the house?*

* * * *

Ethan was hardly earning any money from his job, and we didn't want to keep adding to our credit card debt. So instead of going anywhere significant on a weekend at the end of March, I suggested that we drive into the city and spend a day as tourists. It was not nearly as exciting for me as it was for him, since I was downtown every day during the week. Even then, I rarely ventured out during my lunch breaks. Besides, we admittedly hadn't done much together in Seattle since we'd relocated, which seemed a waste of a perfectly good city.

A coworker recommended driving over the pass to the Yakima Valley to go wine tasting, but that sounded like a long drive and an expensive proposition. A day downtown would have to do.

I considered the Space Needle, but the price just to go up the thing was ridiculous, so I internally vetoed that idea. Instead we planned to check out Discovery Park, Pike Place Market, and an Underground Tour. I found an online coupon for a discount on the tour tickets. *Of course, of course, it was I, the one who was working full time, who found the online discount.* Honestly, I had no idea what Ethan did all day while he was at home. He probably just stared out the window. *Loser.*

All the same, I was trying my best to clear my mind of it all while we drove west on 90 to the city. Leaving North Cloud, we drove through a nasty rain and sleet mix, but as we grew closer to Seattle, it cleared up quite a bit. Normally, I felt instantly better about everything between us as soon as we drove away from the house, but it didn't work this time. I was still feeling aggravated with Ethan. I had never imagined that I would be so disappointed in him.

When we parked and walked around Discovery Park, I was reminded of Stanley Park in Vancouver; they were so similar. Both were surprisingly close to inner city areas, yet both were separated from the rest of the city abutting them and located on inner bays of water. And as I recalled noticing in Stanley Park, in Discovery Park, it was just as easy to forget that a major metropolis was surrounding you.

I was beginning to feel somewhat relaxed. Then Ethan started talking. I didn't want to talk. Not to him, anyway.

A bald eagle soared over our head as we walked along a beach, but I wasn't in the mood to appreciate it. I didn't want to go home, but I didn't want to be walking around the park, either, beautiful as it was. So I told Ethan that I was ready to move on to our next destination of the day: Pike Place Market.

Ethan no doubt sensed I was being distant, but he tried anyway. "It's funny that this is our first visit to this place that is always one of the top associations with Seattle," he commented after we had parked and were entering the marketplace.

I didn't respond, which I knew would bother him. Personally, I thought the top association with the entire area should have been rain. When we began walking through the labyrinth market building, I saw a T-shirt that was pure genius. It had "Seattle" written on it, yet the name was stretched in an arc in order to form an umbrella. *Perfect.* If I had any extra money at all, I would have bought the damned shirt.

Strolling through the market, we learned that the lower floors were nothing too exciting, offering an eclectic array of shops and galleries. However, the biggest draw of these floors had to be that they were so much less crowded than at street level. I'd been told by coworkers that on busy days, the crowds made one feel like a canned sardine, only able to inch forward like one of those disgusting slugs outside our house back in North Cloud. We learned this ourselves on the day we went, as it was a Saturday. But there was definitely a lot more excitement on the street level than the lower levels. The stands lined both sides of the strip and were interspersed with food items, fresh flowers, and local artists and craftsmen selling all sorts of funky stuff.

I imagined there would be more seafood stands, but there were really only a couple. However, at one, they did toss around the fish, to the joy of surrounding tourists snapping photos. I think I saw them doing that on a television commercial once.

After we walked the extent of the market, I decided that it was time for lunch. We should have packed a picnic, and Ethan should have thought of that one, but of course, he hadn't, and instead, we would have to buy something. We walked around for a while, looking for some sort of street food place, but if you didn't count a couple of boring hot dog stands, there really wasn't much. So instead, we were left only with the option of stepping into a restaurant.

Ethan recommended that we should try a teriyaki place. If there was one category of restaurant you could find anywhere in the greater Seattle area, it was a teriyaki restaurant. They were everywhere. Since we had never tried one, I agreed.

I ordered chicken, and Ethan picked beef, mentioning that we could share. I wasn't in a sharing mood with him about anything. But agreeing was better than a conversation. Each plate was quickly served to us with skewers of the meats and sides of veggies and rice. All of the food was good, but I didn't understand why it was such a big deal.

Ethan said something about how the influence must have been from Japanese immigrants, as the region had historically had many. I was sure he realized I didn't want to talk, but he talked on anyway. He added how during World War II, a lot of Japanese immigrants were sent to internment camps. I tried not to listen. I didn't care what he had to say. I turned away from him, pretending to gaze out of the window at the people walking by on the sidewalk, and rolled my eyes.

So you've had the time to look that up, but you don't have time to search for jobs? Or replace that light bulb over the front door that you always say you do, but I know you're lying because it's almost always out? Or to keep the bedroom door open? Or to clean up your shoe prints you obviously leave around the wood burning stove when you bring in wood?

The next and final stop for the day was an Underground Tour in Pioneer Square. By the time we made it over to that side of the city and to the building where the tours began, we apparently had just missed the start of a tour and had to wait a half hour for the next one. Ethan suggested that we have a beer, as the place had its own bar. I gave in because the idea of just sitting there doing nothing for a half hour with him didn't sound remotely enjoyable.

He became surprisingly quiet while we drank our beers, and I imagined he'd finally gotten the point that my annoyance level with him had reached an all-time high. *Finally.*

The guide detailed on the tour that a segment of this neighborhood had been submerged after city officials or someone filled in the area in order to keep it from flooding so often. Something like the entire first floor of every building was then underground, but there were still ways to access it from above. From what our wacky tour guide said, who I was sure was high, a lot of sordid business happened down below.

For the most part, the tour reminded me of walking through different stretches of basements, although it was unique to look up every so often and realize that we were walking directly underneath the sidewalks at street level.

After the tour, we drove back to North Bend. Even though I was blatantly attempting to avoid conversation with him, Ethan tried to talk to me again.

"When I had heard about Seattle's underground before, I had always thought there had been an entire city underneath present day Seattle. But it was really just the Pioneer Square area," he said as drove.

I didn't say anything, but laughed inwardly as the voice in my head called Ethan a dummy.

He then uttered, "Washington State drivers love to tailgate."

"Maybe it's just because you drive too slowly?"

Ethan didn't respond, but I noticed his grip on the steering wheel tighten.

****

So this had turned out to be a really shitty day. First, I thought that, like usual, once we got away from the house, we would return to being a happy couple. Nope, not so much. Not at all, actually.

Lib and I had just had the worst fight of our relationship. We had never fought like that and said such mean things to one another. It was crazy. We were not in control of our emotions or tempers at all. Libby even told me that she was starting to think she would be better off without me—something I never thought I would hear her say, even if she was totally pissed off.

It all started when we pulled into the driveway after returning from spending the day in Seattle and the front door's overhead light was out again. Libby instantly got pissed and demanded to know why I kept refusing to replace the light bulb. When I told her that I just replaced it last week, she blew up at me, calling me lazy, weak, worthless, and a liar. Things only escalated from there. After the fire I started kept going out, she resorted to calling me totally incompetent, leading into her next criticism of my inability to find a job.

I didn't keep my cool. When she called me worthless, I grabbed the first thing within reach, which was a nice vase some friends had given us a wedding present, and smashed it against the wall.

Her spiteful words only enticed my own, and I pointed out that I did whatever I could do to help us around the house and that I did look and apply for jobs on a daily basis. And I couldn't help but add that there were millions of other people looking for jobs, which led her to say something about me not being good enough for her.

This went on for a while, until somehow, we ended up in the laundry room. Out there, we eventually calmed down, and we both realized how cruel we were being to one another, and we both apologized.

In our discussion, we also concluded that the damned house was somehow at the root of our problems, as so much of the tension weighing on our relationship could be traced back to it. In the past, our time away from the house had been good for us, but somehow, the house was now overtaking us, not even letting us escape it. We discussed potentially breaking our lease and moving out. The problem was that we could never afford the penalty we would have to pay for leaving early, nor could we afford to rack up even more debt on our credit cards to cover costs for moving somewhere else. We didn't even have enough cash in our bank account to cover a deposit on a new place.

I held her against me tightly for a long time, feeling her gently sobbing on my shoulder. I reminded her that everyone said that even in bad years, even in the worst years, the weather always would be better in April. And if it was going to be just a little warmer, maybe at least part of our problem with the house would be better. Maybe it would improve our attitudes. She pulled herself away from me slowly and looked at me with moist eyes. Gradually, a small smile crossed her face. She said she wanted to take a shower and go to bed.

I joined her and tried to fall asleep myself, but it was only eight p.m., and I couldn't manage. After I was sure she was soundly asleep, I crept quietly out of bed and returned to my room.

I searched the internet, looking for anything about Mrs. Maul. Maybe if I talked to her and told her about our troubles, she could convince the landlord to let us move out early. She hadn't been the most courteous after our initial encounter, but maybe once she heard of our difficulties in the house, she would feel compassion. It was a lot of maybe, but it was worth a shot. I also hoped to find out something about the history of this fucking house.

After two hours, I gave up and retreated back to the bedroom. I discovered nothing about either topic, but maybe I spent most of that time staring at the walls of the room.

Chapter 7

April

"The weather always gets better in April..." *Whatever.* We were well into the month of April, and it was the same old shit: rain, clouds, cold. I had spent more time on the internet trying to find out anything about the house, but nothing came up, and it probably didn't help that there was really no local newspaper and the community circulator that did exist only had archive editions going back a few years. My search did lead me to discover that the North Bend area was a favorite place of the Green River Killer to dump bodies of women he killed.

I'd decided that since I couldn't find out any information on the house or Mrs. Maul online, I was going to try a different angle. I figured there had to be some sort of Realtor oversight body or something in the state. Perhaps it could help me to track down Cynthia Dixon.

I didn't find exactly what I was looking for, but I did find a number for the Washington State Realtor's Association.

When I called, a young woman's voice answered, saying her name was Brandy.

"Hello, Brandy, my name is Ethan, and I'm hoping you can help me."

She politely answered back, "Hi, Ethan. I hope I can help you, as well."

Good start. "My wife and I are currently renting a house in North Bend, and I'm trying to find out any information I can about Cynthia Dixon, the Realtor who rented it to us. Other properties she is showing or maybe the house's previous tenants."

Brandy was silent on the other end of the line. Eventually, she said, "I'm sorry, but that kind of information is private and not something we can share, even if I could access that information." There was another pause. "Are you having property trouble? Have you contacted your landlord?"

"Well, I think our landlord is one of those out of state people who just bought up a bunch of houses to rent out," I lied. "All we have is a PO Box and an out of date phone number. He's probably some rich guy sitting on a beach in Southern California or something. He's very difficult to reach, and we've not met or had any correspondence with him since we moved, aside from sending him his money every month. So I was really hoping your association would be able to help out." I paused then added, "We're having some trouble."

"Out of state landlords…ugh, those are difficult. Do you have another property manager you could contact?" Brandy asked.

"Yeah, again, I totally understand your suggestion, but the thing is that we had a Realtor show us the place on behalf of the landlord. Our landlord is the property manager, so we're back to that same difficulty in reaching him thing."

"Hmmm, that is a tricky situation," she said. She continued by saying, "Okay, I'm not promising anything, but I may be able to find something out if you give me the name of the Realtor again. Most of the time, they have a file on record with us, listing all of their properties they've been involved with, even when they aren't property managers."

"Great, thanks, Brandy. I really appreciate this."

"You're welcome. I know what it's like to need to reach one of those landlords. Now, what's the name of the Realtor?"

"Cynthia Dixon."

"And you said North Bend, right?"

"Yes, North Bend." She asked for our street address and I gave it to her.

"Okay, I'm going to put you on hold for a few minutes while I search our database."

"No problem."

Classical music blared through my phone, but I didn't mind. In fact, I felt better about myself than I had in months. I was accomplishing something. Libby would be proud of me…maybe…hopefully.

The music stopped, and Brandy got back on the line. "Are you still there, Ethan?"

"Yeah, I'm here."

"Listen, I'm sorry, but I can't really tell you anything."

"Why's that? Did you find any records of Cynthia Dixon and our address?"

"Well, yes, I did. In fact, I see you and your wife listed as current tenants of your address and that Ms. Dixon was involved in leasing of the property to you."

"Anything more?"

"I'm sorry, I really can't tell you anything more. There just isn't much to tell."

I didn't understand. "Brandy, I'm begging you…I'm not asking for you to do anything against the law or to break your association's rules or anything. Anything related to the history of the house? Do you have any of that sort of information available?"

There was another long pause, as Brandy must have been considering my case.

"We really don't have anywhere else to turn," I pleaded.

"Okay, I can tell you that Ms. Dixon was involved in leasing the property to a married couple with children some years back."

"Anything else? Please, Brandy, anything else would be so appreciated." I waited.

I heard her sigh deeply on the other end of the line. "Okay, but this is it. I don't see that Ms. Dixon was at all involved with this property or any other before the previous couple. It looks like she was their property manager. And I can tell you that for some reason, this couple broke their lease within a few months."

"Is there any indication why they did that?"

"I'm sorry, Ethan. That's really all I can tell you."

"How about contact information for Cynthia Dixon?"

"I could if I had it, but I don't. I wish I did. Anyway, I've got to go. Have you contacted the Tenants Union of Washington State? I can get you their contact information, and perhaps they could help you with your issues." Tension was clearly mounting in her voice as she spoke, as if she was growing increasingly nervous.

I thought about the bloody bit of pottery and Libby falling asleep in the tub, the voice she heard. I took the number down, but I already knew I wouldn't call.

"Good luck," she said.

The end of the line went dead. It hadn't been much, but it was a start. It was time for me to talk to the locals.

* * * *

I decided to ask around at the local grocery store. I wanted to see what I could get out people about the house and Cynthia Dixon. The town had a population of only around four thousand people, and all the true locals appeared to know one another. Definitely someone would know of a local Realtor; how many could there possibly have been in the town, after all?

I had looked through my cell phone for the number I had for Mrs. Maul, but I had never saved it, so the search resulted in nothing. Then I went through e-mails I had exchanged with her so many months ago when we began corresponding through a Craigslist posting. I found her phone number in one of the e-mails, but calling the number, I was informed by one of those computer-like voices that the number was no longer in service. Then I attempted to e-mail her, only to have my e-mail returned with a statement that it was an invalid e-mail account.

We also had never actually gone to any office of Mrs. Maul's and instead met her at the house. I could have always tried contacting our landlord, but I didn't have a phone number for him, either; I just had a name and PO Box to send the monthly rent check.

I called the phone number listed on the lease that we were supposed to use in case of a house emergency and received another computer voice telling me that the number was out of service. It was the only item written in ink on the lease aside from our signatures. It looked as if it had been hastily written down, so an incorrect number may have been written.

I wanted to try tracking Maul or Cynthia Dixon or whatever her name was down first anyway. If there was something strange she had withheld about this damned house, she was responsible for not informing us.

"Do you happen to know a local Realtor with a last name of Dixon or who goes by the name Maul?" I asked the grocery teller at the register as he scanned my items. The teller was probably in his mid-forties, but he looked much older. He had a bulging belly, prominent balding head, and had one of those bushy mustaches that were popular in the seventies, from what I'd seen in movies.

"Maul? Nope, never heard of that name before, Realtor or not," he flatly answered without looking at me.

"How about Cynthia Dixon?"

"Nope, not that one, either."

"Are you sure?"

He stopped scanning my groceries and raised his bored eyes in my direction. "Yup, I'm sure."

I forced a grin. "No problem. But do you happen to know where I could find a local Realtor's office that handles rental properties in North Bend?"

The man shrugged his shoulders, now looking annoyed. "I don't even know if there are any local Realtors that do rentals; pretty sure the two Realtors we have in town are only interested in local people buying houses."

I smiled again in response, not letting myself get annoyed by his obvious dig at the "city people" trying to take over the area.

"Whatcha trying to find out?" the kid bagging groceries for my lane abruptly, but not unkindly, asked.

"Actually, I'm mostly trying to find out about our house…" I stopped myself as the cashier raised his eyes at me again. "I mean, about the house my wife and I are renting," I added.

"Well, where's your house?" the bagger kid, who was probably not much older than eighteen, asked.

"Just down the ways a bit on Maloney Grove Avenue. It's an old yellow farmhouse that's been there for around a hundred years." When I described the house, I felt not only the eyes of the cashier turn in my direction, but also from two women in line behind me. I noticed one slowly tilted her head to see me better from behind the other woman.

"Jesus, dude…You don't know?" the bagger kid blurted out, receiving a menacing glance from the cashier.

I was instantly intrigued. "Know what?"

The cashier intervened before the kid could respond, informing me of the total price of my groceries.

I ignored the man. "Please tell me what you know," I begged of the kid.

"Ricky, you know better than to bring the anger of that man down on you and your family," the cashier said to the bagger.

"Ah, forget him. I'm not scared of him like everyone else in North Bend, and he can't do anything to me. He's not even a local any more anyway, living up there with all them other rich people in the Uplands," the bagger kid defiantly responded.

He turned to me and asked, "Do you need help with your groceries out to your car, sir?"

I only had two bags of groceries. "Sure, that would be great," I answered.

The cashier cast a disapproving look at the bagger, but the kid grinned and shrugged his shoulders. "The customer needs help out with his groceries, Bill."

This was one those moments when you had to respect the impertinence of youth.

We stepped outside of the store into a mist-like rain. "I really appreciate whatever you can tell me," I said to the kid.

"Shit...no problem, man," he responded as he handed me the two bags and pulled out a cigarette to light. "I think your landlord is a dickface anyway. He acts like he owns this town just 'cause his family was one of the original ones to settle here. Because of that, his family has always owned a ton of land around North Bend, and he owns more houses than anyone." The kid looked back into the entrance to the grocery store and suggested we start walking toward my vehicle.

"And I think that was pretty shitty of them to let you move into that house without telling you what happened there. That's really fucked up, actually."

My body stiffened in anticipation.

"It was big news in this town like ten years ago or something. Some old lady killed her husband in that house and then killed herself. They were renting, too, like you. Isn't that messed up, man?"

I nodded my head, agreeing, "Yeah, right."

The kid continued, "The house was abandoned after that, and the owners were trying to sell it forever, but no one ever bought it. This all happened when I was still really young, but I grew up not far from there. My friends and I used to run by that house when we were walking down the street. It scared the shit out of us. When we got a little older, we would dare one another to run up and look in the windows. No one ever saw anything 'cause the blinds and curtains were always closed, but it was a fun game all the same."

I thought, *It's no fucking game, kid...this is our lives!* But I didn't say it. I knew he was trying to be helpful, even if slightly untactful about it. "She actually murdered her husband?"

"Well, apparently there was never any real proof that she actually did. There was no way to question her because by the time anyone found out about what happened, she was dead, too."

"So no one really knows for sure if she killed herself, either?"

"Hey, man...from what I remember my parents saying about it years later, the police kept a really tight lid on everything that they found. All I know for sure is that they found them both dead in there, one in each bedroom, and each had been dead a long while before they got there, but both murder and suicide were suspected. There were strange stories that supposedly leaked out from the police department about some weird shit they discovered, but who knows if any of it's true."

"What kind of stories?"

"I don't know, man…It was a long time ago."

"Try to remember, please. Anything at all."

"All right, I remember hearing some shit like the dude was in some spare bedroom or something and the old lady was in the bedroom. The police thought that they had been living in each of the rooms for some reason, like they had locked themselves into each of them. I even heard some crazy shit once that they were like pissing and shitting in buckets in each of their rooms instead of using the bathrooms. Isn't that fucked up?"

I went along with him to try to keep him going. "Yeah, that's really fucked up. Anything else fucked up you remember hearing?"

He thought about it for a moment while he pulled on the cigarette, which somehow stayed lit in the drizzle. "Ah yeah, I remember hearing that the old lady was covered in flies when they found her, but not the old dude. Like he was preserved in the cold. And my old man says that the old guy was famous for going around town in some huge work boots that he wore, even when it was hot as hell in summer. Also, I remember my pops saying that the old man always had on these thick-ass work gloves because he had burned himself on this old wood burning stove so many times that he just kept them on. Pretty odd, huh?"

I felt like telling the kid that there was a lot of oddness in North Bend, but I didn't want to offend my new, and so far helpful, source of information. "Anything else?"

"Well, let's see…I think I remember something like all the clocks in the house were stopped at the same time or something. That's some like creepy fucking stuff, man. And they think she slit his throat with a piece of pottery, 'cause there was like a thick broken ceramic tray found in there near his body."

"But they didn't find a murder weapon?"

The kid shrugged his shoulders, dropped his cigarette and stepped on it. "I don't know, man. You know cops."

Yeah, I know the sheriff. "So did anyone ever have an idea on why the old woman killed her husband?"

"Well, like I said, no one really knows for sure. But I heard my parents talking about it one time with some friends when they thought I wasn't around, and I remember them saying something about that couple having been there for their entire lives, and the woman always wanted a kid, but they could never have one. Apparently, she blamed the old guy and eventually hated him or some shit and killed him for it.

"Anyway, listen, dude, I gotta' get back into work. Glad I could be of help. Don't worry about it: if you've been living there for a while now, then obviously, it's just a house."

"Yeah, right," I said, and a chill ran through my body.

"Where's your car anyway, man?" he asked.

I look around and realized that we were on the far end of the parking lot; I was parked near the front.

"Up there, actually," I said, pointing back toward the store. As we walked, I asked one more question before he disappeared back inside the store. "You said that the house has been totally vacant since the old people died. Are you absolutely sure?"

"Oh shit, you're right, dude. I'm sorry, I totally forgot. There was one couple with some kids that moved in there a couple of years ago or some shit like that. But they only lived there for like a couple of months or something."

"Any idea what happened?"

He shrugged again. "I don't know for sure, man, and no one does. Some problems with their kids or something. People said it was a problem with the mold, like they got sick, but others thought there was something else, something worse. They said one of them flipped out after they got sick, maybe even killed the other one. You know how people talk, saying the little boy killed his sister with some piece of broken pottery just like the old lady did in her husband. But who knows if that shit's real or not."

I felt my stomach turn at the mention of a shard of pottery as the image of the piece I found in the house flashed in my head. "What something else?"

"You got me, man. I gotta go, dude. Bill's a prick, but he'll report my ass if I don't get back in there."

****

Based on the content of her e-mail waiting in my inbox when I returned from my enlightening trip to the grocery store, I opted to hold off saying anything to Libby about the house. She sounded like she was in a pissy mood already. I honestly just didn't want to deal with however she'd react, especially when she was in such a mood.

Her e-mail had zero niceties about it; it was more of a laundry list of orders for me to do around the house. The thing was, though, that I had no problem doing any of the tasks she was telling me to do, but the way she was saying it was not at all pleasant. I guessed that was how marriage was, though—wonderful one day, good the next, bad the day after that, and most of the time, somewhere in between.

Hard to know if it was because of what I'd learned about the house, but at my computer doing research on a blog topic for work, I swore that I heard whispers around me. And I had my headphones on.

When I got up to use the bathroom, I had trouble opening my room's door. There was no way to lock it, but for some reason, the old handle on the door wouldn't turn, and I felt a slight rush of panic as I struggled with it.

I told myself to take a deep breath, that it was all in my imagination...Maybe I just needed to clear my head.

Once I finally got the door open, I walked to the kitchen. While I filled a glass with water in the sink, I stepped on something sharp. It couldn't be, but it looked like that weird pottery shard I had found in the sun room. It was on the floor near the trash can, and it cut my foot right through my sock. I couldn't be certain it was the exact same shard, but it definitely looked like the same one, or a part of it.

I had thrown it away months ago. I clearly remembered dropping it into the trash. *Was it possible that I had missed the trash can? Could it have been there on the floor the entire time?* It was conceivable, but it didn't seem likely.

Could this really be a piece of what the old woman used to kill her husband and herself? Or maybe what the little boy had used to kill his sister? And if it was, it now had my blood on it, as well. What did this mean for Lib and me?

The logical thing to do would have been for me to take it to the sheriff's office, but I didn't feel like having anything more to do with the sheriff after my previous encounters with him. I took it outside to bury near the headless body of Mrs. Pendergrass. It was gone and buried, but I distinctly felt like the damned thing was a little hot when I held it, almost to the point of burning my hand. The slight burning sensation did not quickly go away.

****

"Oh, you have got to be fucking kidding me?" I said.
Ethan shook his head in defeat. "No, I'm not, unfortunately."
"Why didn't you say something to me a couple of days ago?"

"I don't know, Lib. You were in a bad mood earlier this week, and I just wanted to wait until you seemed a little more relaxed," Ethan responded.

"Seriously, Ethan…"

He raised his hands in capitulation. "Okay, okay, you're right. I should have said something earlier. But regardless, there's what I found out."

I was still upset that he hadn't said anything to me about what he had uncovered immediately, but I let it go, as I was much more disturbed by the news itself. "So we're living in a house that hosted a murder/suicide?" Whether based on having just been told this by my husband or not, the house suddenly felt even colder now, if that was possible.

"Well, the kid told me that it was never actually proven. And besides, people die in houses all the time," he replied.

"Yes, but that doesn't mean that they die violently!"

Ethan tried to comfort me by hugging me tightly, and it did help some. But it pissed me off that he was acting like a tough guy. As if he wasn't scared of any of it. He had to be at least a little freaked out by all this.

"Isn't there some requirement that a Realtor inform someone moving into a house if a violent crime had occurred there?" I asked, remembering having heard something like that once.

"Even if that is true, who knows if it applies to a rental situation…and like I said, apparently it was never proven anyway."

"What about contacting Maul and asking her?" I suggested.

"I've tried. I looked through my old e-mails with her and called the number we had for her, but it's no longer in service and her e-mail address is also no longer valid. I asked at the grocery store about her, but no one had ever heard of her. I even looked in a local phone book for any evidence of her, but there's nothing. But like I said, there was a record of her with the state's Realtor association; they had no address for her."

"How about the landlord?"

"The bagger kid told me he lives somewhere in the Uplands and is some sort of local badass around here. I think we can safely assume that he is not going to care about anything we say at this point, and he'll just counter that if we aren't happy we can move out, of course paying the penalty fee for doing so, which I'm sure he would be more than happy to collect from us."

"Yeah, I guess you're right. And we really can't afford that, but

I'm going to talk to my parents to see if they may be able to help."

Ethan added another log to the fire. As he was trying to rearrange the wood burning inside, he scorched his hand on the side of the stove and cried out in pain. I shook my head and said nothing. That would be about his seventh burn so far, and they were forming an ugly collection of scars on his hands and wrists. I'd told him a hundred times to wear gloves when he dealt with the fire, but he never listened.

Ethan ran to the sink and put his hand under cold running water. This was something new. In all the times before he had burned himself, he had never done that. I followed him into the kitchen and looked at his hand. It was a far worse burn, more deep and red than any of the others.

"Don't you think you should wear gloves now?" I asked without looking at his face. When I did look up at him, though, I regretted having been so harsh. He was in pain.

"I don't know how that just happened. My hand was nowhere near the side, and still, somehow, it got burned."

I filled a plastic bag with ice cubes and handed it to him, giving him the *I-told-you-so* look that he should wear gloves regardless.

"How could your parents afford to help us out? They're as middle class as my own," he said after putting the ice bag on his hand.

He was right. My parents wouldn't normally be able to lend us any money, and it was quite possible they would not be able to do so. But my grandmother's passing last year had left them a little bit of money. Although I knew they had been planning to take a trip somewhere since they never went anywhere but to visit me in California, I thought that if I told my mom how bad things had been for us up here, she would consider it.

I told all this to Ethan, and he conceded that this relocation had not turned out great for us on so many levels. We hadn't even been able to establish a group of friends. People up here seemed to be a bit odd to us anyway. Maybe it was the weather.

After dinner, I said that I wanted to go to bed early. Ethan said that he would be happy to join me, which was nice, considering that for the past couple of months, he'd been staying late in his room and there'd been little connection between us. We hadn't had sex in over a month—actually, more like two months, the longest no sex stretch of our relationship by far. Too bad about the terrible cramps and how exhausted I felt. I just wanted to sleep.

****

Perhaps I had cursed myself to a restless night of sleep by mentioning moving out and thinking about it while I tried to fall asleep, as the early-to-bed ploy for a night of sound sleep wasn't happening at all. Instead, I was briefly falling asleep, only to soon thereafter be awoken by some noise. First, it was that windmill nearby shrieking like a metal factory in hell; then it was the sound of mice scurrying in the walls. The mice had gotten worse lately, and I knew that even Ethan was awoken by them at times, as well.

Then I heard what sounded momentarily like someone walking outside our bedroom inside the house. For a second, I totally freaked out. Just as I was about to shake Ethan awake, the sound dissipated. The more I thought about it, the more I decided that it hadn't really sound like footsteps anyway, and I believed I'd even noticed the sound before. It did in a way, but not exactly. It was fairly windy outside, and there was the occasional barrage of rain on the roof as a storm hit North Bend in waves. Most likely it was just the wind from outside forcing drafts through the house.

At 3:33 a.m., I woke up dripping with sweat. I felt broiling hot! Even worse, that disgusting smell had powerfully returned.

I had been in one of those far-too-vivid dreams, where you feel that you are weightless and falling somewhere, only to then be forced awake by a sudden jolting force; most people describe this as the sensation of falling, but I felt like I was being pulled downward. A line of sweat ran down the side of my face like a teardrop.

I turned over to find that Ethan was also apparently awake and had propped himself on his elbows. It was almost as if he was trying to look at something in the darkness of the room.

"Ethan," I said to him, realizing that I was whispering.

He didn't budge at first, and a harsh gust of wind slammed against the side of the house. The windmill sent out some of its most chilling cords of grinding metal to date.

Ethan muttered something about his hand burning. *What the hell did that mean?* I nudged him forcefully and said his name again.

"Whoa, what's going on?" Ethan then replied.

"You were talking in your sleep."

"Sorry," he groggily said. "Anyway, it's really hot in here."

"I know. Did you leave the space heater on in here or the electric blanket too high? It's hot as hell."

"I didn't turn on the heater, and I forgot to plug in the blanket."

We tried to rarely turn on the space heater that we'd bought for the bedroom. Although better than the existing floorboard heaters, it was still a bank account drainer and didn't even manage to warm the entire room. But we had been using the electric blanket quite a bit.

"Were you looking around or something?" I asked him.

"Looking around? What do you mean?"

"Just now, when I woke up, you were on your elbows, like you were looking at something at the foot of the bed or in the room over there," I told him.

"Lib, I don't know what you're talking about. I was totally asleep until you just woke me up."

It was dark in the room, with only a tiny amount of light creeping in through one window from the nearby barn with the horrid windmill. Maybe I had just imagined Ethan sitting up in bed after all. It still seemed creepy.

I was glad thought that he agreed that it was unbearably hot, and he did something we never imagined we would do: opened one of the bedroom windows slightly after ripping away our makeshift weather-proofing seal of packing tape. He said some rain was blowing in through the window, but the alternative of trying to sleep in a sauna was not an option. And the fresh air getting into the room was moving out that awful odor, as well. Ethan didn't say anything about the smell in the room; I'd ask him in the morning about it. He had wrapped an arm around me, and his presence against my body was comforting.

Outside, the wind was howling away, and an occasional gust rattled the blinds of the window that Ethan had opened. I doubted I'd get much sleep in the two hours before it was time for me to get ready for work, but I felt much better with Ethan so close to me.

****

I dropped Libby off at the bus stop as usual. When I returned to the house, there were slugs everywhere around the front door, and there were even more crows around the house than the usual murder that had taken up post outside it. They were perched on the telephone lines above the road, on the top of the house, and lining the wooden fence encompassing the yard. They all seemed to be watching me, and it was unnerving. I hurried back inside to avoid their stares, careful to avoid stepping on one of the fat, slimy slugs scattered everywhere on the ground.

How it had gotten so hot in the bedroom the night before was a mystery, but I must have turned on the space heater in there during the day to warm it up a bit and then left it on all day, and then we hadn't noticed how hot it was when we went to bed because we were both so tired.

The digital clock in my office was blinking when I sat down at my desk, indicating that there must have been a partial power outage, and this could have turned off the space heater in the bedroom.

It had stopped raining—or, as I'd come to learn: there was a temporary reprieve in the rain. No wind blew, but the clouds were dark in the sky. One cloud formation clung to the top of Rattlesnake Ridge, which I could see a small portion of from my room's window. My parents used to always call this the "calm before the storm." I repeated it. It seemed like a storm was heading straight for us.

At the same time I heard myself say this, something odd caught my eye. Leaning closer, I found that there were a few strands of very long brown hair on the corner of my desk. *What the hell?* The hair was much longer than Libby's, and her hair was naturally blonde anyway. And there were a few dead flies scattered around the strands of hair. I thought that the house could not possible get any weirder, but I was proved wrong.

As I lifted my eyes from the desk to the window, I noticed it. It was there in the yard, almost perfectly placed so I would clearly see it once I sat down and looked out at the front yard. The absence of Mrs. Pendergrass's head was no longer a mystery.

But the severed head out there in the yard couldn't possibly be the head of our formerly beloved bunny; that had been months ago, and this head, at least from a distance, looked fairly fresh. And I wouldn't be able to tell the difference between one rabbit head and another.

Logically, if there was some sort of crazed animal on the loose in our vicinity that removed rabbits' heads from their bodies, the same animal had struck again. I'd seen coyotes around more than a few times, hawks had nests in trees surrounding the house, or it could have been an eagle.

Yet still…it was disturbing. *I mean, seriously, what the hell was wrong with this fucking house that death seemed to encompass it?*

* * * *

There was no need for me to look at my phone to see what time it was. I knew. It was 3:33 a.m.

I knew I wasn't imaging it, and I was sure it was the sound of footsteps coming from somewhere inside the house! I was sure of it this time, as there were no mice running in the walls or above us in the attic, no rain pelting the roof, and no wind gusts slamming against the side of the house; I couldn't even hear the ominous grinding of the windmill outside.

It was even hotter in our bedroom than the night before, the stench was stronger than it had ever been, and I felt like I was suffocating. And there were flies in the bedroom. I could feel them landing in my hair. *Flies!*

I tried to talk, but it was like I had cottonmouth and couldn't speak. Even just moving my arm to shake Ethan awake was a supreme effort. When I did, though, I felt that he was already sitting up halfway on his elbows, like he had been the night before.

"I hear it, too," I heard him say softly.

Ethan tried to move out of the bed, but he was struggling. He must have been feeling the same sensation of being paralyzed as me. I still couldn't formulate any words. *Were we both just paralyzed with fear?*

The door to our bedroom, the one we always kept closed at night, was open. Had I heard the handle move? Or was it the light creeping in from a floodlight somewhere on a neighbor's house? But I knew the door was open, and I felt something moving toward us…and it was something cruel. Whatever the presence was, it definitely meant us harm.

The wood paneled walls cracked, as if the room itself was slowly contracting and releasing its own energy. It was dark, but our eyes had adjusted to the darkness, and we both saw it at the foot of our bed, hovering over us…It was the unmistakable outline of a woman!

I couldn't say if she was old or young; I just knew that she was a woman and that she had very long hair streaming down the sides of her shoulders.

The lights in the room suddenly flickered uncontrollably for a few seconds before they all turned on at once.

The woman, or the image of the woman or whatever the hell it was, was gone, and I hysterically screamed as I clung to Ethan's neck, burying my head against his shoulder.

* * * *

Somehow, Libby managed to pull herself together the morning after the event, and she went into work. Although I couldn't blame her, I wasn't looking forward to spending the day in the house, either.

I didn't notice any slugs around, and there were no crows to be seen when we left for the bus stop. It was not raining, or windy, or even as cold as it had been, but just pulling back into the house's driveway made my skin crawl. Lib and I had never been the types to believe in supernatural events, but after last night and everything that had happened, we were converts.

I had always tried to look for an explanation for everything, and maybe some would say we'd just heard some noises and freaked out when the power flickered off and on and imagined the whole thing. Even if that theory had some reason, it would not explain the overwhelming and threatening presence both of us undeniably perceived last night. *And how could we have both imagined seeing the same ghost?* There had just been too much weird stuff happening in the house for it all to be entirely disassociated.

Before dropping her off, Libby and I went to a drive-through espresso stand, which were everywhere, and sat in the car talking before her bus arrived. I revealed to her all of the things I had held back from telling her before in fear of scaring her, such as finding a rabbit's head outside my room's window.

In turn, Libby told me how she had experienced another terrifying bathtub experience and how she could not even look in the tub's direction when she was in her bathroom. She had started keeping the bathroom door pried open with a bronze statue of Buddha one of our friends had given us after a trip to Northern India. I had noticed the statue but never said anything to her about it. With our perceivable lack of communication for the last few months, it didn't seem that important.

Our discussion then turned to the apparition itself. We'd seen enough movies to know that we were facing a hostile ghost that didn't want us in the house; fake or not, all the ghost stories in the world were based on something. And it was clear that this thing didn't want us in the house and would continue tormenting us, or worse. This was no "Casper" we were dealing with.

We had no explanation why the severity of its presence had been so unpredictable. Why, for instance, why had strange events occurred sporadically? And why had we only seen what was apparently the woman who had murdered her husband in the house? Wasn't he there as well, as evidenced by the boot prints left on the floor that Libby had just told me about? Perhaps each presence had been responsible for different incidents? After all, if the couple had not gotten along in life, culminating with the woman killing the man and then herself, it was hard to believe they would coordinate their haunting of us in death.

Regardless, there was no disputing that things in the house were worse now than ever. And considering what it did to Libby in the bathtub when we first moved in, there was no way of predicting what harm this presence or multiple presences were capable of inflicting on us.

Libby didn't want me to return to the house, but I told her I was going back to start packing some suitcases and bags and that afterward, I'd go find a cheap hotel for us. Libby pointed out that I could use her laptop so that I could still be available to work at the hotel in the meantime while we figured out what to do. It was a great suggestion, as returning during the day to work on my desktop computer was not something I wanted to do. Contrary to what's often portrayed in movies, we were not one of those crazy couples that stayed in a house once they were sure it was haunted. We collectively agreed on this one: hell had obviously claimed the house, and hell could have it back.

Lib planned to call her parents right away. She was then going to talk to her boss about our situation. She didn't say it, but I knew her well enough to know that she wouldn't completely reveal what had been happening, though I imagined she'd be convincing enough for anyone to feel sympathy for her. She told me that she would call me as soon as she could.

So, I was back at the yellow house on Maloney Grove. No more calling it "our" house now. When I first saw this place, I really liked the looks of it, but now, I couldn't imagine why I ever had. With its general aged appearance and the creepy window above the front door, the place fit the definition of spooky. I glanced upward at Mount Si. It had dark wispy clouds around it, but I could still make out its peak looming over me. At one time, I had thought the mountain to be watching over us in a positive way. I no longer felt the same.

I took a few deep breaths before opening the front door and stepping inside. No whoosh of air passed by as I did. I saw no blurred image move across the television set. I heard no doors slam. No cupboards banged shut. And the temperature didn't rapidly fluctuate (it was bitter cold, as normal). I didn't even smell the awful stench that we now knew was attributable to something much fouler.

But I felt a persistent malevolent presence in the house. It was still watching me. Now I knew that I'd often sensed it while sitting in the office; it was the same overbearing pressure Libby and I had both felt last night when it openly revealed itself to us. Something was alive in this house.

I tried to keep my strength and courage up, despite the chill coursing through my body. I felt like I had a terrible case of the shakes that compounded into one single pulsation, constantly throbbing. Breathing was difficult, and my pulse was soaring, but I managed to flip on a light switch and was relieved to at least have light in the room.

Quickly as I could, I opened all of the blinds and curtains, turned on every light, and propped every door of the house open with anything I could find that was heavy enough to hold back anything but an extremely forceful push. I was compelled to announce out loud that I was only going to be there for a few moments and that we wouldn't be returning, but it wasn't necessary. This thing was everywhere, watching me somehow. It knew.

My only hope was that my presence could be tolerated long enough for me to gather a few things without provoking another attack. As I started back toward the bedroom, I turned on the lights in the in-between room and felt petrified for a moment as I noticed that the hardwood floor in the room was covered with the outline of footprints, with a defined focus of them directly outside of the bedroom door. The footprints were the impression that would be left by a man's large work boot.

I wiped away the tears that were involuntarily falling down the front of my cheeks and hurriedly packed a couple of suitcases and a few bags, hardly noticing what I was placing in each.

****

"Ethan, my parents said they would be happy to loan us as much as we may need. Apparently, my grandma was a shifty old lady and had stashed more cash than anyone was ever aware of until after she was gone. And they are fine with us paying them back whenever we can; they just want us to be out of that house and safe," Libby said to me excitedly over the phone.

After leaving the house, I drove to a small motel near downtown that was fairly rundown and nothing fancy, but it would do. There wasn't much of an option for overnight lodging to begin with, but being a slow time of the year, the mom and pop run place was more than happy to book us a room for the night. The older couples' eyes grew wide when I mentioned that we may be staying for a week or more. They had no problem with me checking in early, and I collapsed on top of the bed as soon as I entered our room. I felt drained and exhausted, but hearing Libby's voice was uplifting.

"And there's more. I think instead of moving into another place up here, let's just move back to California. I mean, let's admit it: things haven't quite worked out for us up here like we hoped. This thing with the house...well, it just solidifies in my mind that we aren't and never were meant to be here to begin with, so let's just go back to where we know we will be happy living. I know we wanted to try living in a different place before we settled down, but we have now, and now there's nothing to hold us from going back."

Libby was talking in rapid-fire mode, and I was having trouble keeping up.

"And as far as where we could live, I called my friend Melissa; you know, the one that is still in school and lives with her boyfriend? Anyway, they are renting a house, and she says they have a nice livable basement and that we can stay there with them as long as we need until we find our own place. And don't worry, it's a pretty new house, and they say there's nothing at all creepy about it."

My mind was still groggy, but before I said anything, Lib jumped back at it.

"And as for my job, I talked to my manager, and although she's going to have to let me go, she said that I can work remotely for the company for another month. So I also called my old boss from my internship during grad school. He said that they are actually looking to bring someone else on board full-time within the next couple of months, and he was very excited to hear that we are going to be moving back. It's perfect!

"Everyone up here always says just wait until the day after the Fourth of July, when summer begins. That then it'll be nice until after Labor Day. But I don't want to wait until July or wait until next month for something better. And if this house is haunted, who knows how many others might be, as well? Let's just get the hell away from here…far away."

Clearly, Libby had made up her mind for both of us, and I agreed with her completely.

Chapter 8

May

We only stayed another week in the state of Washington after the first night in the hotel. In that time, we devoted ourselves to making all the necessary arrangements to move. We arranged for a moving company to show up at that house, pack everything, and move it down to California, where they would store it for us until we were able to get our own place again. We found a moving company to pack our belongings without us actually being there while they did. Ethan merely went over and unlocked the house to let them in and returned to lock it at the end of the day when they were done. He told me that he did not set one foot inside the house.

"So our so-called landlord was kind of an asshole when I called him and told him about our situation and that we were going to move out early," Ethan said.

"How so?" I asked.

"Well, it just seemed like he wasn't surprised or at all concerned about our predicament. And I don't know..." His voice trailed off.

"Ethan...tell me."

"Well, it just seemed to me as if us leaving quietly was somehow a favor to him, and we obviously know it has nothing to do with him getting more money from us to do so. Maybe the way he sees it is that if we leave quietly, there won't be any new rumors around town about the house, and he'll be able to keep renting it out forever and collecting his monthly rent checks."

"That does make sense. From all that you learned about that house, he's probably glad to see us go sooner rather than later."

That night, I began having intense cramps and pain. I really wanted to have sex with Ethan, feeling so much relief about being out of that house, but I still didn't really feel in the mood.

When I called my mom the next morning and described it to her, she laughed and congratulated me. She made a big deal of saying how the loan they were giving us would help to pay for clothing, a crib, a stroller, and all sorts of other baby stuff.

* * * *

Driving south, I felt warmer with each passing mile. As we passed about halfway through Oregon, we felt sunshine gently touch our faces, and even though we still had a long drive ahead of us, it felt like we were returning home.

Only one thing still troubled me. I really hoped I wasn't pregnant. Ethan and I had not had sex for so long…it was odd that I would not have felt the beginning stages of it long before. And if we had conceived in that evil house…I couldn't think of it. The thought made me sick, accompanied by clutching my stomach in pain and feeling intensely nauseous as we crossed the border into California.

Our first moment back in California was nothing like I had imagined it to be. Instead of pulling over to the side of the road to hug and kiss and look forward to our future together, I told Ethan to pull over for a different reason. He held me steady as I wretched on the side of the highway. I felt like I was going to die. And I wondered if we'd ever truly escape from the yellow house on Maloney Grove.

Printed in Great Britain
by Amazon